The Evil That Men Do

Detective Inspector Jeremy Faro is a happy man. His stepson Dr Vincent Beaumarcher Laurie is to marry the charming Grace Langweil of Priorsfield House, a much-respected Edinburgh family. And Vince is not the only person in love, for Faro is extremely taken with the beautiful Barbara Langweil, Grace's aunt.

Faro and Vince are invited to a sumptuous meal, all prepared and served with the meticulous attention which makes dining with this devoted family such a gastronomic delight. The only flaw is the obvious ill-health of Grace's father, Cedric. Can this be dismissed as mere over-indulgence in a well-stocked cellar?

The very next day, however, Faro learns of Cedric Langweil's sudden death and his own dream of happy families threatens to collapse like a pack of cards as his young stepson faces the most terrible dilemma of his professional career.

The post-mortem on Cedric Langweil reveals evidence of arsenic poisoning, and it is no consolation to Faro to recognize that in the particular province of murder detection lie his greatest skills: skills which he must exercise to the fullest extent of his powers, regardless of the fact that the murderer must be a member of the dead man's family, with whom both he and his stepson are intimately concerned. As Faro's investigations uncover deep-seated family rivalries and sinister secrets, death strikes the fated family yet again before the abominable truth is finally laid bare.

THE EVIL THAT MEN DO

An Inspector Faro Mystery

ALANNA KNIGHT

MACMILLAN
LONDON

First published 1993 by Macmillan London Limited

a division of Pan Macmillan Publishers Limited
Cavaye Place London SW10 9PG
and Basingstoke

Associated companies throughout the world

ISBN 0–333–57524–5

9 8 7 6 5 4 3 2 1

A CIP catalogue record for this book is available from
the British Library

Phototypeset by Intype, London
Printed in Great Britain by
Mackays of Chatham PLC, Kent

For
Ernest Kirkby

Chapter One

Detective Inspector Jeremy Faro was a contented man. Life was good and not even the approach of his forty-third birthday could detract from the pleasurable anticipation of the next few months.

He didn't feel middle aged. As he buttoned his dress shirt in his bedroom in Sheridan Place, he would, had he been a vain man, have accepted the evidence of his own eyes and the admiring glances of those of his acquaintance. True, the once fair hair was thinly streaked with grey, but this enhanced rather than diminished the powerful Viking image of a born leader, a king among men.

Now, as he tied his cravat, he whistled under his breath. Yes, life was good indeed and he had a strange feeling that lately things were getting better not worse in the Edinburgh City Police. It was six months since he had dealt with a murder case and he was almost persuaded that human nature had taken a turn for the better.

He smiled wryly at such an idea. If things continued like this he would be out of a job.

But his sense of satisfaction was more personal. Next week would see the end of his long separation from the elder of his two daughters. Fifteen-year-old Rose was to enrol at the Grange Academy for Young Ladies, with special instruction in Languages of All Kinds; Emily, who was two years younger, would remain in Orkney meantime.

Faro sighed. With Rose at home, he would be a family man again without the last desperate measure of taking a wife. For he could never rid himself of the guilty awareness that policemen made poor husbands and that his neglect had contributed in no small measure to his dear Lizzie's death.

Had his powers of observation and deduction encompassed his own four walls he might have realized that her health was too frail for the pregnancy that killed her – and took to the grave with her the son he had craved.

But Lizzie had left him a stepson and no father could wish for a better son than Dr Vincent Beaumarcher Laurie – a son who also fulfilled the role of companion and colleague.

In the spring one of Faro's long-cherished dreams would come true when Vince married Grace, niece of Theodore Langweil of Priorsfield House, his present destination. It was also the home of his own secret love. Ridiculous at my age, he told himself, blushing like a schoolboy . . .

As he closed his front door in Sheridan Place he recalled with gratification Grace's indignation at the merest hint that Vince's stepfather should move into a separate establishment.

'We will try it out for a year or two,' she said with a shy look at Vince, 'and if – if we need nurseries and so forth, then we will move into a larger house.' And taking his hand, 'But you will come with us. No, sir, I will have none of your arguments.'

Faro knew that they were useless in any case since Grace was a strong-willed modern young lady with a mind of her own.

The Langweils continued the old-fashioned custom of dining at four o'clock. As he walked the familiar mile from Newington to Wester Duddingston, he thought of the many less happy occasions when he had travelled this road in urgent pursuit of criminals. Rarely had he leisure to admire the gloaming, that curious stillness when the trees and buildings are sharply outlined against an azure sky and the very earth stands still.

Now the magic of a winter afternoon was enhanced by

a rising moon, and from the loch three swans took flight, the sound of their wings audible, birds from an ancient legend come to life.

Then, silence restored, his ringing footsteps were the only sound in the wine-clear air as he thrust open the iron gates leading into the drive of Priorsfield House.

Birthplace of Langweil Ales Limited, the simple tower-house of centuries past had been enlarged in the eighteenth century. Overlooking the loch, tradition (which the Langweils were anxious to perpetuate) claimed that it had all begun with a humble medieval alehouse patronized by the kings of Scotland out hunting in the dense forest on the slopes of Arthur's Seat.

Perhaps this romantic and colourful notion had some roots in history, for the name Langweil had drifted in and out of local records. But whether Mary Queen of Scots had stayed there benighted by a snowstorm on her way to Craigmillar Castle and whether Bonnie Prince Charlie had supped there in a secret rendezvous awaiting the arrival of French gold to support his cause were matters for conjecture only.

What was undeniable, however, was that the Langweil fortunes had dwindled until Grandfather Langweil discovered an old recipe for ecclesiastical ale, reputedly served by the monks of Kelso who had owned the lands of Duddingston in the twelfth century.

Grandfather Theodore's recipe flourished. He bought a disused mill on the Water of Leith whereupon Langweil Ales became a redolent part of the western approaches to the city and Priorsfield Inn became Priorsfield House as successful ventures into port wine and claret swiftly followed.

The Langweils bore an unsmirched reputation, not least as philanthropists whose names appeared on all the distinguished guest lists and charitable societies; and their loyalty to past Scottish monarchs was acknowledged by the coat of arms of HRH Albert, Prince of Wales, who was partial not only to Langweil Ales, but to the liqueur, their latest production, which he had graciously endorsed.

9

Grandfather Theodore was less successful in a recipe for raising children. His one surviving son produced four sons and a daughter. The eldest, Justin, a sickly infant and invalidish child, was followed two years later by Theodore, then Cedric. A decade of stillbirths followed before the safe arrival of Adrian.

As an adult Justin's deteriorating health meant that survival depended on living far from Edinburgh's cruel climate. In the 1850s he departed for North America where he promptly severed all connection with the family.

'In fact,' Vince had said, 'they don't know whether Justin is alive or dead, which might make complications in the matter of inheritance. I mean, suppose a son or daughter walked in some day and claimed the Langweil fortune,' he added anxiously.

Faro had smiled wryly. Theodore's first wife had died in childbirth long ago. If his second marriage and Adrian's first were without issue then Grace would inherit the Langweil fortune, including two breweries and two very large houses.

'I shouldn't bank on your future wife's expectations,' Faro warned him good-humouredly. 'Theodore's young wife looks healthy enough and so does Adrian's.'

'Barbara is touching thirty and they have been married for twelve years,' Vince reminded him. 'Offspring don't sound very likely.'

'I imagine Adrian and Freda might yet produce a quiver of bairns to carry on the Langweil name.'

'After six years? Do you really think so?'

Faro pondered. Six years *was* a long time for a couple who allegedly wanted a family.

'Besides I sometimes think Adrian's ruling passion for the golf course leaves him little time or energy for the more important things in life,' said Vince.

'Be careful that ruling passion, as you call it, doesn't also become yours,' Faro warned the newest victim of golfing fever.

Vince grinned sheepishly. Hitherto a reluctant morning riser, he now dashed off to play nine holes with Dr Adrian before their first patients arrived at the surgery. In his role as Cupid in Vince's romance, Adrian's word was sacrosanct.

The two doctors had met at a colleague's wedding in Aberdeen where Adrian was in general practice. Returning to Edinburgh for family reasons last year, Adrian had promptly invited Vince to set up his brass plate alongside his own.

The wheel of fortune that was to change all their lives having been thus set in motion, it was no time at all before Vince, invited to Priorsfield, sat next to Cedric's daughter Grace, and fell in love. This was in no way a remarkable or unusual event since Vince was particularly susceptible to pretty girls. Except that this time fate took a hand.

The lady in question was equally entranced by the handsome young doctor and the rejoicing from both their families was mutual and spontaneous. The Langweils were known for their lack of side; 'a man's a man for a' that' could have been their motto on their coat of arms, if they had chosen such niceties. Although Vince was illegitimate, and his stepfather a 'common policeman' who had risen through the ranks to become detective inspector, such social limitations aroused no feelings of resentment. After all, the liberal-minded Langweils were proud to claim descent from an alehouse keeper.

As Faro climbed the front steps of Priorsfield he looked back towards Edinburgh. The twilight sky was dominated by the silhouettes of Salisbury Crags on one side and the Pentland Hills on the other. Not lacking in imagination, he still found it difficult to realize that Duddingston, now so accessible to the new villas on the rapidly developing south side of the city, had, according to the historians, once been covered by the dense Caledonian forest now as extinct as the volcanic origins of Arthur's Seat. There, legend claimed, in a hidden cave the valiant king whose name it bore slept with his true knights, awaiting the clarion call that never came.

The Romans had marched here, and with the Christian

11

era came the priory lands. In relatively modern times, the armies of King Edward of England, of Cromwell, and of Bonnie Prince Charlie had stumbled along the once inaccessible cart track now transformed into Queen's Drive, a handsome carriage road from the royal residence of Holyrood Palace where it frequently bore illustrious guests to dine with the Langweils.

The imposing mansion was considerably more ancient than the Gothic towers and turrets which had been added fifty years ago. In the fast fading light the sky was bright with a thousand stars and a pale moon touched the ancient central block and throwing into sharp relief corbie stepped gables and gun loops, a grim reminder that Priorsfield had survived dangerous times when this part of Edinburgh was a wilderness threatened by wild beasts and wilder men. After the Jacobite forces' defeat at Culloden, rumour had it, the Langweils had 'bought their way' into the favours of King George II and had so remained intact while other royalists, dispossessed, saw their men ride into exile or execution in Edinburgh's Grassmarket.

As Faro waited for the door bell to be answered, he remembered something Vince had said only recently. 'As you told me long ago, Stepfather, and as you've never allowed me to forget, history is written by the victors.'

'Or rewritten, if they're clever enough to destroy the original records,' had been his laconic response. But he little knew how he would have cause to remember his words.

Now he heard footsteps and returned his thoughts to the present, and to a living example of this very situation. The door was opened by Gimmond, the butler, who greeted Faro politely and removed his cape and top hat. Only the merest flicker of an eyebrow would have revealed to the observant that the two men were old acquaintances. Gimmond, or 'Jim Gim' as he was better known, had been involved in shady dealings, and his common-law wife, a known prostitute, had died in mysterious circumstances. He was saved from the hangman's

12

rope by Faro's evidence and the Scottish verdict of 'Not Proven'. A verdict which those concerned with justice wryly dismissed as 'We know you did it, go away and don't do it again.' Five years had passed and Faro, on his first visit to Priorsfield, had recognized Gimmond who, with his second wife, was now respectably established as butler and housekeeper. Gimmond's relief had been considerable when he realized that Faro was not going to 'shop' him with 'the boss'. Faro's philosophy, unlike many of his colleagues, did not subscribe to 'once a murderer, always a murderer'. He considered in the case of the *crime passionel* that this was unlikely to recur and believed profoundly that men and women can be re-shaped for better as well as worse by bitter experience.

Now he followed Gimmond across the vast panelled hall and up a great winged oak staircase, its landing adorned with ancient tattered flags and rusted armour, proud mementoes of battles long ago. Alongside were portraits of generations of past Langweils and a fine rare painting of Bonnie Prince Charlie, his modern-day royal successors represented by an imposing array of signed photographic portraits. Such displays, Vince informed him, were essential for any well-off family who were going anywhere and had pretensions towards aristocratic connections.

As Faro approached the drawing room, voices raised in heated but friendly argument were hastily hushed as Gimmond announced him.

Grace, with a beaming Vince at her side, rushed forward to introduce a middle-aged man wearing a clerical collar.

'Meet our second cousin, Stephen Aynsley.' And as the two men shook hands, 'Stephen has just arrived from America.'

'Not quite, my dear. I have been in Scotland several months now. In St Andrews, where I recently took holy orders,' Stephen explained with a shy fond smile in Grace's direction. 'I have only recently had the pleasure of making the acquaintance of my charming family.'

13

All this information surprised Faro since Aynsley looked considerably more mature than the usual run of students nearer Theodore in age than Adrian. Stoop-shouldered, presumably from carrying the cares of the world, with the skeletal thinness of the aesthete, Stephen, he was informed, was son of Grandfather Langweil's only sister Eveline.

Little of the Langweil good looks had descended by the distaff side, Faro decided. Learning that Aynsley was shortly to leave for missionary work in the unexplored regions of Africa, he realized that a superabundance of the Langweil famed zeal and enterprise more than compensated for this deficiency.

The second stranger was Piers Strong. Introduced as an architect, Faro suspected that his agitated manner and heated complexion concerned the yellowish documents he clutched so anxiously and were possibly the cause of the argument he had interrupted.

'Congratulations, Stepfather,' muttered Vince. 'You arrived just in time.'

'Nonsense, Vince. Blood hasn't been spilt yet,' said Theodore. And to Faro, 'We are merely trying to sort out whether to have or to have not some new alterations and additions to the house. Vince has given me to understand that you are a traditionalist, so I am relying on you to take our side.'

Traditionalist, eh? Vince's quick glance in his step-father's direction pronounced that word as a rather less flattering 'old-fashioned'.

'My dear sister-in-law here' – with a gesture in the direction of Grace's mother Maud, Theodore continued – 'has succeeded in tearing the town house apart and now, aided and abetted by young Adrian and Freda, with their infernal notions about hygiene, they are directing their missionary zeal – beg pardon, Stephen – towards Priorsfield. All I say is what was good enough for my grandfather – and his grandfather – is good enough for me.'

'Rubbish, brother. Rubbish,' said Adrian. 'Bathrooms

and water closets are an absolute necessity if we are to stay healthy. I'm sure Barbara as a modern young woman will agree.'

Barbara. Where was she?

Faro had known on first entering the room that she was not there. Now at the sound of her light step outside the door he turned and once again felt as if he had been thumped hard in the chest by a sledge hammer.

She came straight to him, took his hand. 'Welcome, Mr Faro, it is good to see you again. I trust you are well.'

Faro stammered something appropriate in reply, conscious that he was blushing like a lovesick lad. Then she was gone.

'I have spoken to Mrs Gimmond as you suggested, Theo.' And to Adrian: 'And what is this I am to agree about?'

Feasting his eyes, his whole being upon her as Adrian reiterated the argument, Faro was amazed that the rest of the company were oblivious of her effect upon him. She was so strikingly lovely. Quite the most beautiful woman he had ever seen. Not only in the composition of her looks, but the essence of womanhood without which, he knew, good looks are as dead as the portraits that stared down from the walls.

Again he found it difficult to realize that she was touching thirty. She could have passed for eighteen. Here was a woman who would grow more beautiful with time's passing. Like Shakespeare's Cleopatra whom 'age cannot wither, nor custom stale her infinite variety'.

He suppressed a sigh. She was not for him, could never be for him. But every man has his own fantasy, his own goddess, and Barbara Langweil was his.

Drawn once again into the round of domesticity, the argument resumed over the merits of a bathroom, Faro observed that Barbara's smile contained a nervous glance at Theodore.

'Oh come now, I'm sure you'd appreciate more than one bath a week,' said Adrian.

'Well, I do manage that—'

15

'I dare say you do, with the maids carrying pails of hot water upstairs.'

'Um – yes.'

'That was good enough for most folk,' Theodore repeated.

'Not that old story again, Theo, for Heaven's sake. Come on, Cedric, you haven't contributed much to this argument. Aren't you going to support me?'

All eyes turned in Cedric's direction. But the enthusiasm of the converted was strangely lacking. Sighing, almost wearily, he said: 'You had better ask Maud. I leave matters involving the household to her. And I stay quietly out of sight when the builders move in.'

Maud laughed. 'But you did approve of the results, didn't you, dear? Be fair, now. You spend more time in the bathroom than any of us.'

Cedric shrugged. 'Yes, I have to be honest. I approved of the result. Once the dust cleared.'

'There, you've admitted it, Cedric,' Adrian said triumphantly.

Vince had complained to Faro that the serenity of the fifty-year-old town house in Charlotte Square had lately been shattered by a tide of architects and builders. One of the fine houses built by Robert Adam, it fell short only in lacking one of the indoor bathrooms now *de rigueur* for well-off families.

The Georgians had been content to deal with the natural functions by a commode behind the screen in the dining room and one under the bed for more intimate occasions, but those who could afford to be health conscious in modern Edinburgh now produced written evidence to add to their arguments.

'The spread of disease,' they claimed, 'undoubtedly begins in the home, where matters of hygiene can no longer be ignored.'

'Dammit, Cedric,' Adrian persisted, 'you told me that life had never been so good. So why don't you convince our stubborn brother here?'

'Priorsfield is his business, not mine.'

16

Adrian sighed wearily and turned again to Theodore. 'Think of the advantages. You have more rooms than you know what to do with. What about HRH's ablutions when he visits? He's a heavy drinker, after all.'

'I get your meaning, but we do have a water closet, you know that perfectly well,' said Theodore stiffly.

'One wc. In a house this size,' said Adrian. 'And what does our architect think about that?'

Piers looked anxiously at Theodore. 'As Dr Langweil has pointed out, sir, this is not just a matter of vain extravagance. This ever-growing city of ours desperately needs up-to-date sanitation.' Having begun nervously, the architect now gathered the strength of conviction. 'And healthy citizens need more than efficient drains in the streets—'

'They do indeed,' said Adrian. 'We don't want any more outbreaks of cholera and typhoid. Isn't that right, Vince?'

Faro felt that his stepson would rather have been left out of this domestic argument, torn between pleasing his senior partner and displeasing Grace's uncle, as well as his future father-in-law.

'There are problems, quite serious ones, sir,' Vince said to Theodore. 'Ones I know you are fully aware of. All this new building on the south side, the villas in Duddingston' – he pointed vaguely – 'have created new problems. For Priorsfield too.'

When Theodore did not respond, Vince went on. 'The rats which haunted the old Nor Loch have now taken refuge in newer buildings. A regular plague of them, which the city fathers are anxious to conceal, especially since the building of the railway station.'

'And with the rats go our worst diseases, we are sure of that,' said Adrian.

Turning his back on his brother, Theodore indicated Piers Strong, who having raised this hornets' nest, now shuffled miserably from foot to foot.

'Can't we leave this discussion until later, Adrian? Hardly fair to our guest—'

Piers regarded him gratefully.

'Or to Mr Faro—'

At that moment the dinner gong sounded.

'Splendid,' said Theodore, in tones of relief. 'Saved by the bell. Shall we proceed?'

As the family, now chattering happily, made their way in the direction of the dining room Faro, hoping to escort Barbara, found she was claimed by Stephen, and offered his arm to Grace's mother. Half-way downstairs, Maud exclaimed: 'Oh, I have left my fan upstairs. Bother. Oh would you, please? Bless you.'

As Faro ran lightly upstairs, the drawing-room door was open. Theodore was leaning forward, his hand gripping Cedric's shoulder.

'Look, I only invited the fellow here because you said he wanted to see over the house. Nothing more,' he added heavily. Suddenly aware of Faro's presence, he swung round and with a startled look almost guiltily released his hold of Cedric. 'Just telling him that what I do in my own house is my business. Don't you agree?'

Faro smiled. 'It's a gentleman's privilege after all.'

Following the two brothers downstairs, the scene he had witnessed, with its air of urgency, their strained faces, had a menacing quality which stubbornly remained, filling him with strange uneasiness.

Uneasiness very soon to be justified.

Chapter Two

In the dining room, the candle-lit table could not be faulted. Silver and crystal gleamed, mahogany shone, there were skilfully arranged exotic flowers from the greenhouses on which Theodore prided himself.

Not only was the table exquisite but so too were the Langweil family. Almost, thought Faro, as if they had been chosen especially to grace the setting. Such a gathering gave him a vicarious sense of family pride, for as an only son, left fatherless in infancy, close kin was a commodity he had in very short supply.

The two brothers Theodore and Cedric had the perfection of features commonly associated with Greek gods, Cedric's unusual pallor accentuating the likeness to alabaster statues.

Of that handsome trio, Adrian's looks were most outstanding. Despite his intensive personal research into the effects of chloroform and dangerous excursions into new methods of alleviating human suffering, his complexion was radiant. Doubtless those hours on the golf course were responsible.

Looking across the table at Freda, his plump and pretty young wife, Faro realized that the strongest likelihood was that Adrian's branch of the family would eventually succeed if, as seemed likely, Theodore and Barbara remained childless.

Barbara. Faro found his gaze drifting back to her constantly, unable to linger, sure that he carried his heart in his eyes for this woman with all the ethereal beauty of an angel from a Botticelli painting. He found himself wondering uncharitably if Theodore had chosen her with the same meticulous care as he had collected the other adornments of his house.

Looking round the table he saw that he was not alone in his admiration. Each time she spoke, every male head turned eagerly in her direction. Her voice, with its slight American accent, was beautiful and unusual. Although she spoke rarely and only a little above a whisper, that was enough to still all other conversation.

Theodore obviously adored her. He had brought her home – 'captured her' as he called it – from one of his rare visits to New York. A fortunate man indeed. And Faro sighed at the game of chance that was life itself.

If Theodore had chosen for outstanding beauty, the same could not be said of Cedric. If Barbara's looks suggested the purity of a painted angel, Maud's finely boned features merely suggested a washed-out water colour abandoned by an indifferent artist.

He saw Vince glancing in her direction and wondered if the same thoughts were going through his stepson's mind. For this was an oft-discussed topic between them: why many handsome men chose plain wives. Vince called it the 'peacock syndrome', a kind of vanity whereby a man's own good looks were enhanced by a plain mate.

At his side, Grace was smiling across into Vince's eyes. A well-matched couple who gave the lie to Vince's theory, thought Faro with some satisfaction. Grace had inherited her father's exotic Langweil looks.

Piers Strong sat next to Vince and having discovered a sympathetic ear was waxing eloquent on the latest development in domestic sanitation and the city sewage systems.

Faro listened with some amusement to a monologue not entirely suitable for the dining table, but delivered with the same missionary zeal that Stephen Aynsley was expounding to Maud on heathen Africans.

'He has worked wonders with our house,' whispered Grace. At Faro's startled glance, she giggled.

'Not Stephen, Piers, I mean. Even Uncle Theodore

was impressed with our two bathrooms. I can't imagine why he's so stubborn about making changes here.'

Faro smiled. Vince had told him that as a subject of admiration, visiting guests to Cedric's home were now taken directly upstairs to view and acclaim these new masterpieces of elegant plumbing.

'A little more wine, sir.'

Allowing Gimmond to refill his glass, Faro sat back in his chair. Listening to the gentle arguments, the laughter and teasing, the family jokes, he felt extremely well-blessed.

Vince had done well, very well indeed. Much better than his earlier less fortunate ventures into prospective matrimony had suggested, and Faro thrust from his thoughts the disastrous choices that had blighted Vince in the past. As for his own fears that a young wife might have objections to a stepfather sharing their establishment, Grace could not have made it clearer that instead of losing a stepson he was gaining a stepdaughter.

Game soup and salmon had been followed by roast goose and a dessert of plum pudding. An excellent meal prepared and served with the meticulous attention to individual taste that made dining at Priorsfield House a gastronomic delight.

Only one apparently meaningless incident threw a faint shadow on that evening. Cedric twice retired hastily from the table in the middle of the meat and the dessert courses. Looks were exchanged but the company was too polite to do more than acknowledge his return.

To a whispered question from Maud, he said: 'Yes, of course, I'm all right, m'dear.' And leaning over he patted his daughter's hand. 'I've been celebrating rather too well before we sat down to dinner.'

Faro glanced round the table and caught a long look exchanged between Theodore and Adrian while Barbara studied her plate rather too intently, he thought, than the situation merited. Then without any further glance in Cedric's direction, hastily the brothers resumed the general conversation. This deliberate ignoring of Cedric struck a false note somehow. As if they were all too well aware of the cause of his withdrawal.

And Faro, well used to interpreting his own observations, felt uneasily that there was perhaps more in that moment of shared anxiety than could be justified by mere overindulgence in the Langweil cellars.

At last Barbara stood up. 'Shall we adjourn for coffee?'

This was a new innovation which had Faro's full approval. The Langweils on all but the most formal occasions had dispensed with the custom of gentlemen remaining to enjoy their port and cigars apart from the ladies.

The company followed into the upstairs parlour, a welcoming withdrawing room with rose velvet curtains and a glowing fire. Here the family visitors usually spent their evenings together, reading and listening to Barbara play the piano.

At Faro's side, Piers said: 'We are now in the oldest part of the house. This is the central block, the old towerhouse.' And tapping his foot on the floor, 'Below us are the foundations of the original alehouse.' To Theodore he added: 'I suppose you realize, sir, that according to the original plans and the Session Records, this room was once considerably larger than it is now.'

The position of the fireplace, set two-thirds of the way along the wall, instead of centrally as was customary, was out of symmetry: a curiosity which had often jarred on Faro's earlier visits.

'One of Grandfather's alterations last century,' said Theodore.

'I don't think so, sir. Pardon me if I disagree but it is much more recent. When I was last here with Mrs Langweil and Mr Cedric—'

'While I was absent in Glasgow, of course,' said Theodore shortly with a veiled glance in his wife's direction.

'My dear, it was merely—' Barbara began.

As usual she was not allowed to complete the sentence.

Theodore patted her arm. 'I'm not blaming you, my dear, of course I'm not,' he added, with a gentle smile at her anxious expression.

'I merely thought, sir,' Piers put in, 'that this room, adjoining the drawing room, would have been in the old days the laird's study, or the master bedroom. However there is something not quite right.' And tapping his foot on the floor, 'There's a ten-foot discrepancy in the original plans which I've had access to. You may be interested in seeing them—'

'No necd,' said Theodore shortly. 'I'm fully aware that the room has been altered at some earlier stage. You know what it's like in these old houses, full of odd twists and turns. I'm sure you'll find some cupboards on a later plan that have been dismantled to enlarge the rooms.'

Piers was not to be put off. He continued eagerly: 'I believe you were born here, sir.'

'Indeed, as were all the family.'

'Then these changes must have been quite recent. In your childhood even. Perhaps you've forgotten?'

'No. I have already told you,' Theodore said coldly. 'There has been nothing done to this room.' And with a gesture, 'Not even decoration that I can recall.'

Piers turned hopefully towards Cedric, who shook his head.

'My brother is younger than I am,' said Theodore.

Cedric smiled. 'I expect it was in our Papa's day.'

'But that isn't possible, sir. The wallpaper—'

'Ah, here's the coffee. At last,' said Theodore, his relieved tone indicating boredom with the architect and his intensity.

The evening over, Faro and Vince declined the offer of a carriage in favour of walking the short distance home to Sheridan Place.

'We are thinking of a honeymoon in Paris,' said Vince. 'Are you pleased?'

'I am indeed, lad. It's great news. Hey, slow down. You're walking too fast.'

'You're out of condition, Stepfather. Have to get you out on the golf course. Nine holes before breakfast. That'll get you in perfect trim in no time.'

'I get enough exercise,' grumbled Faro, 'without chasing a blasted ball around a green.'

'You don't know what you're missing. Marvellous for the digestive system. A necessity after dining at Priorsfield.'

'Indeed, another memorable meal, but a little too rich for your future father-in-law. I can sympathize with him.'

'I didn't think he looked at all well,' said Vince.

'True. Very pale, I thought earlier in the evening.'

'You noticed that too.'

'I think you should recommend a few rounds of your golf to put some colour back in his cheeks.'

'As a matter of fact I am rather worried about him.'

'My dear lad, I've seen you just as bad – worse even – after a night out at Rutherford's—'

'It's more than that, Stepfather. This isn't the first time he's had to leave the table hurriedly during dinner. A weak digestion, he calls it.'

'And what does Adrian call it?'

'Oh, he gives him a bottle to help and grumbles that families with doctors never want to listen to their advice.'

Faro's own digestive system was not his strong point and he could understand Cedric's impatience. Especially as Vince's attempts to coddle him, as he called it, drove him to distraction.

'You know what he's talking about,' Vince added with a grin.

'I do indeed, but I don't usually have to take flight from the dining table in the middle of a meal.' Faro had long ago diagnosed his stomach upsets as due to the stress of a detective's life, with hasty, infrequent, and often inedible meals. Doubtless, Langweil Ales had their anxious business moments too.

But that look he had interpreted between Theodore and Cedric, as if they shared some secret awareness, continued to haunt him. It came to mind vividly when next day a constable brought into the Central Office a note from Vince.

24

Stepfather. Prepare yourself for a shock. Cedric died during the night. I am going to Priorsfield.

Faro carried the news into Superintendent McIntosh's office.

'Can't believe it, Faro. Saw him only yesterday morning. Seemed perfectly fine in wind and limb.'

When Faro told him about the dinner party, McIntosh shrugged.

'No one dies of indigestion. Doubtless his doctor brother will know the real cause.'

As they left together, the newsboys on the High Street were calling: 'Sudden Death of Cedric Langweil. Read all about it.'

Buying a paper, with McIntosh staring over his shoulder, Faro was somewhat frustrated to find only a heavily black-edged paragraph giving Cedric's age and brief biographical details.

'That's how they sell newspapers,' grumbled McIntosh.

As they parted and Faro headed home towards Sheridan Place, a series of melancholy pictures filled his thoughts. There would be a funeral, followed by six months' deep mourning for the family, before the marriage of Grace to Vince Laurie could now take place.

Suddenly the world of happy families he had pictured to himself only yesterday was no longer a reality. Ominously he felt it was in danger of collapsing like a house of cards.

Anxious for news he waited up until midnight but Vince did not return until breakfast the following morning.

'Grace is inconsolable. As for her poor mother – the whole family are absolutely shocked. It seems quite unbelievable. None of them could have imagined such a catastrophe.'

Faro agreed sadly. In the tragedy of personal grief, Vince the doctor had been obliterated by Vince the lover, momentarily refusing to accept that the symptoms of indigestion could be also those of heart failure.

'Men do drop dead in the street every day, in what seems like healthy middle age,' Faro reminded him gently. 'And women too. I thought you might be used by now to sudden deaths, lad. It's only when it comes close to home, it's so very hard to bear—'

'If only you were right, Stepfather,' Vince groaned. 'But it's worse, much worse than you imagined.'

'In what way, worse? Sit down, lad. Come along now, have some breakfast.'

Vince went instead to the sideboard and poured himself a whisky.

'No. I need this more,' he said and huddled exhausted over the fire. 'I was expected to sign the death certificate.'

'He was a patient of yours? Not Adrian's?'

'A member of the family cannot sign the death certificate, you know that. Anyway, Adrian asked me to attend the whole family, for purely minor ailments, since they refused to take him seriously. You know how it is. They all seemed exceedingly healthy and I never had more than a cough bottle to make up for any of them. As for Cedric, he was adamant that he never saw doctors, especially siblings or their partners. All he has ever asked for was a prescription for his indigestion.'

'Which you dispensed?'

'No. Adrian always made it up.' Vince drained his glass and stared miserably at him. 'I did the routine death examination while Theodore stood at my elbow. I knew that he found it painful and he was very anxious that I sign the certificate and get it over with.'

Pausing, he shook his head. 'Then I knew I couldn't do it. There was something wrong.'

'Wrong?'

Vince nodded. 'Very wrong. You see, I was quite certain that I wasn't looking at a man who had died of a sudden heart attack.'

'Then what—'

Vince shook his head. 'Nor did he die of a massive dose of indigestion. As I examined him I had an uneasy suspicion that I was looking at a man who had died of poisoning. I've seen it all too often, those discoloured and inflamed patches on his skin, particularly over his abdomen. And I learned from Maud that what he politely called indigestion for the family's sake, was in fact chronic and persistent vomiting and diarrhoea.'

With a sigh he added, 'I hardly need to have the Marsh Test done on this one, Stepfather. The symptoms are unmistakable. Cedric died of arsenic poisoning.'

Chapter Three

'I'm notifying the Procurator Fiscal,' said Vince, 'there will have to be a post-mortem. You can imagine all the trouble that is going to get me into, hinting that my future father-in-law's death was not due to natural causes.'

If this was to be a murder enquiry, which Faro also dreaded, for inevitably the investigation would land on his desk, then he had better save time by getting certain facts in the right order.

'You said Theodore was standing at your elbow. Surely you mean Adrian?'

'No. Adrian was away at Musselburgh at the crack of dawn. He's practising for a club championship, and of course that—'

'Wait a moment. You said, at the crack of dawn. Hold on, lad. Let's go back to the beginning. When did Cedric die?'

'During the night. They stayed at Priorsfield, as you know.'

'Was that unusual?'

'Not at all. They frequently do so after a dinner party.'

'And so Maud made the unfortunate discovery this morning, after Adrian had left for the golf course. How very distressing for her.'

'No, no. Early morning ritual is that the maid leaves trays outside the bedroom doors at seven o'clock and Maud noticed Cedric's was still there on her way down to breakfast at nine—'

'Wait a moment. Are you implying that Maud was not sleeping with Cedric that night?'

28

'Exactly. She was sharing with Grace. You see, Grace refuses to sleep alone at Priorsfield. When she was a little girl she had, well, rather a scaring experience.'

Vince seemed reluctant to continue and Faro prompted him:

'What happened?'

'She – thought – she saw a ghost. It wasn't just a dream because it happened more than once,' he added hastily. 'Everyone knows that small children often fancy they see things. I know it sounds ridiculous –'

'Not to me, it doesn't.'

Vince smiled. 'Of course, you're sympathetic, aren't you. Well, this will interest you. She always described his white bagwig and old-fashioned knee breeches – and how he walked straight through the wall.'

'And who was this spectre supposed to be? Any ideas?'

'From his dress, I should say the French officer who came to deliver the gold to Prince Charlie while he was preparing for the Battle of Prestonpans. The gold that might have changed the face of Scottish history.'

'One of many similar legends, I should say, of gold hidden and lost for ever.'

'Rather different in this case. The French count's ship came too late, pursued by ill luck, an English frigate, and then a storm. He arrived in Leith after Charles Edward had departed. Then rumour takes over. The alehouse keeper at their rendezvous, the original Langweil, if truth be told, got rid of him as he slept. Poisoned him and when things went against the Jacobites used the gold to bribe himself into Butcher Cumberland's favour.'

'I don't think people give much credence to such rumours. But the whole thing was revived, Cedric told me, much to his family's distress when a skeleton was dug up in the grounds during the last century with a knife blade between its ribs.'

'Probably one of the Prince's gallant soldiers who had fallen foul of a drinking companion. People have very romantic imaginations, especially when it comes to historical misdeeds. No doubt Cedric had told Grace the story when she was quite small and she had dreamed the rest.'

'I agree. I think that is most likely the reason. Anyway it made quite an impression on her. Now she insists that her mother share her room.' Vince looked at Faro. 'You know, I was quite surprised when she told me she thought Priorsfield was haunted. Especially as Grace is such a sensible, practical sort of girl.' He sighed. 'How did I get on to all this?'

'You were telling me that Maud noticed the untouched tray outside Cedric's room as she went down to breakfast at nine.' Faro thought for a moment. 'But she didn't look into the room. Wasn't she curious?'

'Not at all. Theodore and Cedric boasted that they needed little sleep and they rarely retired before three. As on this occasion when they decided to polish off another bottle of Langweil claret as a nightcap.'

'Did they indeed?' said Faro significantly.

'No, no, Stepfather. It couldn't have been in the claret otherwise Theodore would have been poisoned too—'

'Unless the arsenic was added to Cedric's glass only.'

Vince registered astonishment. 'But that would mean – Theodore—'

Faro said nothing. But a demon in his brain said only one thing. If Theodore had murdered his brother for cause or causes still unknown, then he would hang.

And Barbara – Barbara will be free—

'You are wrong, Stepfather.' Vince interrupted his giddy tide of fantasy. 'It cannot be Theodore. I'll never believe that—'

'We won't know whether I'm right or wrong until we get all the facts together in their right order and see what we have left over. So at what time did Maud finally go into Cedric's bedroom?'

'About eleven o'clock. They had an engagement in Edinburgh for lunch. Of course, she was in a terrible state of shock and Theodore raised the alarm immediately. The coachman was sent for me and when I arrived nearly an hour later I knew from the state of his body – rigor mortis had set in – that he had already been dead for several hours.'

'So the breakfast tray couldn't have been tampered with. Therefore his brother had been the last to see him alive – after they'd finished off that bottle together.'

'Surely you can't believe that? Why, they are devoted to each other —'

Faro cut short his protests. 'I'm trying to concentrate only on the facts. What you found when you got to Priorsfield. Namely, Cedric was dead and his brother anxious for you to sign the death certificate —'

He had hardly finished when the doorbell rang. The two men exchanged glances and, looking out of the window, Faro saw that the caller was Grace Langweil.

Mrs Brook ushered her into the drawing room. Throwing down her gloves, ignoring Faro, she rushed across to Vince.

'What is all this about? Uncle Adrian tells me that – that you made a great fuss over the – the – certificate for poor dear Papa. And that you refused to sign it. Refused,' she repeated, eyes wide in astonishment. 'Now they tell me that you are insisting that there must be a post-mortem. Vince – Vince, what in God's name has got into you? Are you mad or something?'

Suddenly she broke down sobbing and Vince took her into his arms. But she refused to be comforted and pulling away from him demanded: 'How could you be so cruel. How could you do this to Mama and me? And to our family who have always treated you with such kindness?'

'It has to be done, Grace.' Vince's voice sounded hollow.

'Has to? I don't understand "has to". I know about post-mortems. Surely you could permit my father' – she emphasized the words – '*my father* to go to his grave without carving up his poor body. Surely you owe us that much.'

Over his shoulder Vince gave a despairing glance at Faro who quietly left the unhappy pair. He saw them leave the house together, unspeaking, their faces pale, stony.

31

Shortly afterwards he departed on the train to investigate a fraud case near Musselburgh. Its intricacies kept his mind and energies away from the scene he had left at Sheridan Place and when he returned home late that evening, Vince was still absent.

At midnight his eyes drooped with weariness. It had been a long and gruelling day and he was glad to retire. Sleep was not to be his, however; he was alert at every sound, every footstep or carriage outside the house that might indicate Vince's return.

One thought refused to leave his mind. If Theodore was innocent, who then in that apparently devoted family should wish to poison Cedric Langweil? All evidence must incriminate the last person who had poured him a glass of wine, who was apparently the last one to see him alive.

Faro found himself hoping for a miracle, that the post-mortem would prove Vince's misgivings were wrong, for he knew his stepson too well not to understand the anguish this decision had given him. To go against the whole assembled family of the girl he was to marry and declare that her father and their beloved brother had not died of natural causes.

Dawn was breaking, the first birds cheeping in the garden, when at last he drifted off into an uneasy slumber.

At the breakfast table Mrs Brook had a message for him. 'A lad has just handed in this note from Mr Vince, sir.'

Detained on a confinement case. Theodore would like us both to present ourselves at Priorsfield at four o'clock this afternoon.

In happier circumstances Faro would have enjoyed the walk to Wester Duddingston. There were swans gliding on the loch's mirrored surface and in the pale muted sunshine he stopped at a vantage point to gaze back at where a dwarfed castle crouched like a heraldic beast on a horizon misted with the approach of day's end. This was his favourite hour, his favourite aspect of Edinburgh.

A city of dreams and a city of nightmares where the past walked close to the present. Close your eyes and you could sense that the past was alive and that history was still happening.

As he approached the gates of Priorsfield with its lawns rolling down to meet the rushes of Duddingston Loch, a skein of geese moved overhead, their faint cries filling the still air with a melancholy sweetness as they circled to feed on the rich sandbanks of the River Forth.

To think that mere hours ago he had approached this house with such hopes and optimism for the future. Already it seemed like part of another happier world, and, filled with sudden ominous dread for what lay ahead, he wondered as he walked up the front steps whether any of them would again be so happy and carefree as that last fateful dinner party, with no greater problem than whether or not to install a new bathroom.

Vince had already arrived. And taking him by the arm, he said:

'They're upstairs, in the drawing room.'

The family were assembled, waiting; silent, subdued under the curious numbness of sudden and unexpected bereavement. Their funereal blacks contrasted strangely with the garden glowing under the approach of sunset. In the shrubbery a robin added his plaintive winter song and a blackbird's warning cry was lost in the strident screech of one of the Priorsfield peacocks.

With a slight bow in Faro's direction Theodore stood up and with his back to the fire addressed them, his manner little different from that used to point out some approaching crisis to the shareholders of Langweil Ales.

'Since Dr Laurie has cast doubt on the probable cause of my brother's unfortunate death, as head of the family I have asked you to be present on this occasion to put on record that we are all in agreement that a post-mortem, however regrettable and distasteful to us, must be carried out. Before the matter proceeds any further there are certain other matters involved.' Pausing he looked directly at Faro. 'You get my meaning, Inspector.'

The formal address left no doubt whatever in Faro's

mind as Theodore continued: 'I mean, of course, that following notification to the Procurator Fiscal, a police investigation might ensue into the possible cause of Cedric's death.'

A shocked silence followed an outbreak of whispered comments. Anxious looks were exchanged and angrier hurt looks directed towards Faro.

A moment later Theodore continued: 'I think we should make it plain to the Inspector that all of us, with the exception of Grace here' – he looked across with gentle compassion to where she huddled close to her mother's side, clutching her hand for comfort – 'all of us present can verify that Cedric's death was not in the least unexpected.'

Heads were nodded in agreement as he turned again towards Faro. 'My brother was in fact gravely ill. Dying. We have all been sadly aware that for the past six months he was suffering from an incurable brain disease and that his days were numbered.'

'Oh no, no.' The cry was from Grace and Maud put her arms around her. 'Hush, darling. Hush.'

'No, Mama, it can't be—'

'My darling, I assure you it was. But your happiness was his main concern, we were to keep it from you—' Maud's voice failed and as she sobbed quietly Theodore went over and took Grace's hands.

'Dearest child. It was your papa's earnest wish to spare you, his only child, so that you would prepare in joy for your wedding, and even that he would still be with us and well enough to lead you down the aisle.'

'Oh Papa, dear Papa,' Grace sobbed. Now it was Vince's turn to reach out for her, but turning from him she clung to her mother.

'Naturally this secrecy he imposed upon us all has been a great strain,' said Theodore. 'Especially Adrian—'

Faro and Vince looked quickly at Adrian, who nodded slowly as Theodore went on: 'He did not wish to involve his own brother, I'm sure the reasons are only too obvious and painful to need any further explanation.'

34

'He asked me to recommend another physician,' said Adrian. 'I suggested he consult Wiseman in Heriot Row.'

'Who will confirm all I have told you,' said Theodore to Faro. 'I am sure this will put your mind at rest when Wiseman gives you details of the magnitude of my brother's illness.' Then, to Vince: 'Although we can heartily commend Dr Laurie's integrity and need for absolute truth and scrupulous accuracy, the result was unfortunately a little ill timed without being in full possession of the true facts leading to my brother's death.'

His thin-lipped smile and slight bow in Vince's direction contained, Faro thought, not a little barely concealed resentment.

'Since Mr Cedric was consulting Dr Wiseman, why was he not called upon to sign the death certificate?' Vince demanded sharply.

Theodore sighed. 'He was. But unfortunately for us, as he was at a family wedding in Ireland and neither available nor immediately accessible, it seemed the most natural thing in the world that Dr Laurie, as our family physician, should perform this merely routine task—'

'If you had thought to inform me, sir—' Vince began desperately, and turning to his partner, 'Or you, Adrian,' he added accusingly.

Theodore spread his hands wide. 'Gentlemen, gentlemen. What's done is done. No one is to blame.'

Pausing he glanced at the clock significantly and then addressed Vince and Faro. 'There is much to do. I am sure you will both appreciate that this is a difficult time for us.'

As they rose to leave, accompanied by Adrian, Theodore added: 'I'm sure we can rely on your discretion not to make the unhappy circumstances of my brother's death more painful for us than is absolutely necessary. And now we have important family business matters to discuss. Our lawyer Mr Moulton will be arriving shortly. Perhaps you will excuse us?'

In the hall an elderly man, white haired, bearded, his slightly built frame exuding an air of authority, was handing his cape and tall hat to Gimmond. Faro's first thought was that he was an undertaker by the solemnity of his attire.

'Good day to you, Dr Langweil,' he addressed Adrian. 'Permit me to take this opportunity to express the sincere condolences of our establishment on the sad loss of your brother, and indeed to all the family. Such empty places—'

Adrian cut short the threatened eulogy, which promised to be lengthy, with a bow. 'Thank you, Mr Moulton. I believe Theodore is awaiting you in the drawing room.'

The lawyer's manner seemed to crumple. 'Oh, indeed,' he said nervously. 'If you will excuse me, gentlemen,' he added and walked quickly upstairs.

'What a bore the man is,' whispered Adrian, catching up with Faro and Vince who had reached the front door. 'We used to call him Old Mouldy when we were children. His documents are even wordier than he is.' Then taking Vince's arm, he said: 'If only you'd mentioned your suspicions to me, I could have cleared up all this unfortunate business at once.'

'I doubt that,' was Vince's short reply.

'For Heaven's sake, I had no idea that was what was in your mind when you wouldn't sign the death certificate. I thought, fool that I was, that it was because you regarded it as not right and proper – since you were – almost – one of the family—'

And so Cedric Langweil's body was interred in the family vault at Greyfriars Kirk with all the pomp and splendour attributable to a high-ranking citizen. It was one of the largest funerals Edinburgh had ever witnessed and brought crowds of sightseers into the High Street. St Giles was tightly packed and the funeral oration, conducted by Reverend Stephen Aynsley, as cousin of the deceased, told of 'a grave illness courageously borne and kept secret from all but the members of his own family'.

While all this was happening in the public eye, Cedric Langweil's main organs were being subjected to the

Marsh Test for arsenic, carried out in the police laboratory at Surgeons' Hall.

Vince awaited the results with some apprehension, finding himself in a now totally unenviable position, made to feel by his future wife's family that he had let them down badly.

'They've done so much for me, and now the way they look at me, the coldness in their attitudes, makes me feel as if I've betrayed them. The hint is that I have brought their good name into disrepute and have also heartlessly besmirched the reputation of a dying man.'

'Surely Grace believes in your good intentions,' said Faro.

'Of course. The dear girl is loyal to me, but she is naturally torn by the deep-rooted image of her devoted family. Then of course, there is her poor mother's anguish. It's worse for her than any of them. Damn it, if only I had signed the wretched certificate and let it go at that. If only Adrian had told me that Cedric was dying anyway, I could have accepted that he had taken his own life.'

Faro looked at his stepson in shocked surprise. 'Vince, lad, you couldn't do that. It's against everything you've ever believed in. Sign a declaration that might be false—'

'I know, I know. But now there is so much at stake. My own personal happiness and Grace's. We love each other, but now I see this scandal of her father's death will always be between us. A dark shadow.'

'A shadow that time will erase, when two people love each other,' said Faro soothingly, aware that his voice carried little personal conviction.

Twenty-four hours later his suspicions were proved right. Vince returned to Sheridan Place and threw down the report of the post-mortem on the table in front of him. 'Well, Stepfather, it seems I was right to trust my instincts and observations, scant good that they will do me. There was no trace of a brain disease or any other evidence of ill-health. His heart and lungs were sound. In fact, what-

37

ever the Langweils' claim, Cedric was a healthy man in the prime of life who might reasonably have expected to live for another thirty years.' Vince sighed. 'I had actually been hoping that he had some incurable illness and had taken his own life. But not now. Someone is lying,' he added heavily.

The same thought had been running through Faro's mind.

Now, putting his hand on the report, Vince regarded him solemnly. 'According to this, the stomach contents revealed that Cedric Langweil died of arsenic poisoning. He had in fact six times the normal fatal dose.'

So their worst fears were realized.

'I dread to think how this will affect me. And Grace. As for you, Stepfather, it looks as if you might well have a murder investigation on your hands.'

This was a situation Faro knew only too well. After the post-mortem, the verdict of cause of death; and then all the heavy machinery of criminal investigation by the Edinburgh City Police would go into immediate action, as personified by Detective Inspector Faro.

Someone had poisoned Cedric Langweil. Faro had no doubt that whoever spread the rumour that Cedric was dying was also his murderer. In the present case, clues to the identity of the killer were painfully easy to follow. And sooner rather than later the guilty person must be run to earth, charged, brought to trial. And hanged by the neck.

No other way, no way of escaping or forestalling the law's mechanism existed. And it was no consolation to Faro to recognize that in the particular province of murder detection lay his greatest skills. Skills which he must exercise to the full extent of his powers regardless of the fact that he and his stepson were both intimately concerned not only with the guilty but also with the innocent members of the murdered man's family.

He had not the least doubt, nor he guessed had Vince, that Cedric Langweil's killer would be unmasked with a minimum of effort, found where poisoners were almost always found, in the bosom of that apparently devoted family circle.

There was no pride in knowing that there was only one prime suspect to follow. When he was brought to trial the sufferings of the other Langweils would be intense as their emotions and motives were laid bare and subjected to enquiry and careful scrutiny. For the guilty man's motive, he did not doubt, would not have changed since Cain had killed his brother Abel. Gain, or jealousy or secret resentment that had festered over many years.

What secrets were they about to unlock? Faro wondered. And how would their revelation affect, distort, or change for ever the hopes of marriage between Vince and Grace?

Knowing that in his hands lay the outcome of an investigation calculated to destroy all hopes of two young people's happiness, Detective Inspector Jeremy Faro was a profoundly unhappy man.

Chapter Four

On being informed that Dr Wiseman was expected back in Edinburgh later that day, Vince and Faro set off to call upon Theodore Langweil.

'If only we could have seen Wiseman first,' said Vince. 'This is most unfortunate.'

The visit to Priorsfield at least promised to be both painful and brief.

Faro observed Theodore Langweil narrowly as he read the post-mortem report on his brother. His expression remained impassive. Although his hands shook as he laid it aside, such reaction was understandable, and his lips moved silently, as if repeating the monstrous conclusions of the report.

A beloved brother murdered.

Bewildered he gazed helplessly from Faro to Vince and back again. Then he shook his head several times like a man awakening from a dreadful nightmare as he searched for some explanation.

'I cannot understand this at all. It is as I told you,' he said dully. 'We all knew that Cedric had been seriously ill, fatally ill, for the last six months. Wiseman will confirm that, whatever this wretched piece of paper says. Why don't you ask him?'

Vince said: 'There is one possible explanation, sir. Knowing that he was dying, could he not have taken his own life?'

'Impossible. I could never entertain such a thought, not for one moment. He was a courageous man. And he would never have done such a thing. He loved life.' Silent

40

for a moment, he looked towards the window with its darkening clouds.

'The fact that it was to be short made it even more precious. He was determined to live it to the utmost. "Every minute of every hour of every day, Theo." Those were his very words to me, here in this room.'

'What about pain, sir?' asked Vince gently. 'Was he not afraid that he might suffer a great deal?'

'He had learned to live with blinding headaches. He told us the consultant had assured him that with the help of a little morphine – near the end – the end would be speedy, total collapse, a coma, days only. But you are no doubt aware of all this, surely, Dr Laurie,' he added irritably.

Vince nodded. 'It rather depends upon the exact location of the tumour.'

With a sigh Theodore continued. 'I know of one very good reason why Cedric would not have taken his own life. There was a very large insurance taken out at the time of Grace's birth and this, as you know, would be forfeit if he had taken his own life.'

Looking at their faces, he said, 'I see you are not convinced, but I have one other reason for believing that he did not intend to die. There were important documents awaiting his signature.' He tapped a drawer. 'They are still here in my desk.'

'May I ask what was the nature of these documents?' Faro asked.

'Transfer of business shares. Oh, nothing serious. We were merely selling some properties. I can assure you that we are not in danger of bankruptcy.' Staring again towards the window, he frowned. 'He also talked of revising his will.'

'In what way revising?' said Faro sharply. In his experience changed wills were frequently the cause of mysterious and totally unexpected family fatalities.

'I am not at liberty to discuss such matters at present,' was the scornful reply. 'But I can tell you that the clauses under discussion related to the family business concerns only. I hope all this information satisfies you.'

It did not satisfy Faro at all, but presumably Theodore was now aware that in the event of a murder enquiry – should he, as the prime suspect, be accused of his brother's murder – then such information and more, much more, painful information must be laid bare.

Theodore left his desk and indicating that the interview was over, held open the door for them. 'I leave to your imagination the embarrassment to say nothing of the distress your somewhat over-conscientious behaviour has caused this family in their time of sorrow and bereavement.'

Oh, Barbara, Faro thought. If only I could spare you the humiliation, the grief of all that is to follow. Not only Barbara, but Grace too. And Vince.

For although Theodore's remark applied to both men, his resentful glance sliding off Vince held this impulsive young doctor his niece was to marry directly responsible for this dread blight on the Langweil name.

'There are a lot of things that require explanation,' said Faro as they walked homewards, breaking the long silence between them, for Vince wrapped in his own despair had not yet given thought to the shortcomings in Theodore's statement.

'First of all, what I still fail to understand is why Adrian did not warn you of Cedric's condition.'

'Loyalty to the family and all that, I suppose. You must remember, Stepfather, that he wasn't expecting Cedric's end to be by poisoning either.'

'What about this prescription Adrian gave him?'

'For indigestion, you mean?'

'Yes, how often would he take a dose of it?'

'Whenever he had an attack. I imagine. Or if attacks were persistent, then last thing at night.'

'Then doubtless he took at least one dose during or after the dinner party.'

'I should imagine he would have done that, yes. Hold on, Stepfather,' Vince laughed uneasily. 'You're not suggesting that Adrian's simple mixture—'

'I'm only suggesting from the facts known to us that the poison was administered sometime before Cedric retired at three o'clock. Either in a glass of wine or in a spoonful of medicine.'

'Meaning that the chief suspects are now Theodore and Adrian. Is that what you are suggesting?'

'Or Maud. Or one of the staff. Oh, I don't know, lad. All I'm indicating is that we are only at the beginning and we need to know a lot more about those critical last hours Cedric spent at Priorsfield. Did he really believe he was dying, or did someone persuade him that he was a doomed man?'

'Our only hope is Dr Wiseman. We've met on the golf course. Let's hope he'll be able to throw some light on this wretched business.'

Outside his house, Dr Wiseman was paying off the carriage which had brought him and his travelling bag from the railway station.

Faro's first impression was of a younger man than the affluent middle-aged consultant he had expected to meet. Or perhaps, he thought wryly, like policemen, doctors gave the illusion that as one got older, they got younger.

His confidence in the interview was also blighted by realization that their arrival was most inopportune. Wiseman appeared very put out and agitated, especially when he learned the nature of Dr Laurie's visit and that he was accompanied by a police detective.

'Yes, indeed, I read about Mr Cedric Langweil's death in the London newspapers when I got back from Ireland.'

When they showed no signs of departing he invited them into the house with certain reluctance watching the maid carrying his luggage upstairs. Finally he ushered them into what appeared as a bleak and inhospitable consulting room.

'Please take a seat, gentlemen. What can I do for you?'

'We need some information about your patient, Doctor,' said Faro.

Dr Wiseman was trying hard not to tremble. 'What kind of information?'

'Dr Langweil has given us to understand that his brother consulted you.'

Dr Wiseman frowned. 'Yes, I believe so,' he said vaguely.

'Then perhaps you knew something of his case history.'

'Case history?' he repeated warily.

'We understand from the family that Cedric Langweil was incurably ill, that he had a disease of the brain,' said Vince, 'and that he had only a short while to live.'

Dr Wiseman's bewildered glance went from Vince to Faro and back again. 'I'm sorry to hear that, gentlemen. Very sorry indeed.' And shaking his head, 'What you say may be true, but it is new to me. I assure you he never consulted me about any such condition. Your informant is mistaken. It must have been some other physician.'

'Are you sure?' demanded Vince.

'I am indeed. As I am personally acquainted with Dr Adrian and have had the honour of attending various members of the family, it is unlikely that I would not have remembered such an illustrious patient as Cedric Langweil.'

Dr Wisemen smiled and in his expression Faro detected relief. Somehow this was not what he had been expecting.

'I do apologize for having seemed so vague when you asked me about him. You see, I think I only saw Cedric professionally once and that was when he had a festered thumb. I have attended Miss Langweil and her mother on one or two trivial medical matters.'

'You don't know then who he might have consulted?'

'I'm sorry, I haven't the least idea. But surely Mrs Langweil would be the one to ask.'

A now very cheerful Dr Wiseman saw them to the door, his parting remarks about the coming golf championship and comforting words on the present state of Vince's handicap. With an early meeting proposed between two doctors, they shook hands and parted most cordially.

As they headed towards Princes Street, Vince said: 'I don't know about you, Stepfather, but I'm completely baffled. Why on earth did Cedric lie to his family about Wiseman? A complete waste of time, and very embarrassing for a colleague, I can tell you. And we're not one whit wiser now than we were before.'

But Faro remembering Wiseman's anxiety had his own thoughts on the matter. 'I wonder who is lying. You realize, lad, that in the circumstances, with no evidence apart from his family's insistence that Cedric was a dying man, we now have no other option than to treat this as a murder case.'

At the Central Office, Superintendent McIntosh wasn't at all pleased by this turn of events as he threw down the post-mortem report on to his desk and regarded Faro darkly across the table.

'This is your province, Faro, and frankly not one I envy you. Dashed difficult I know, with your stepson almost a member of the family. And the Langweils respected pillars of society. I'm afraid this is going to create one hell of a scandal.'

McIntosh's feelings were understandable, since he too had enjoyed the Langweil hospitality at Priorsfield over a number of years.

'If only we hadn't brought in the Fiscal,' he sighed. 'I suppose we could have ignored it. Presumed that the poor chap had taken his own life. Not unusual in the circumstances for a dying man to be unable to face up to the last weeks—'

'Look here, sir,' Faro interrupted, 'you know as well as I do that if Langweil was poisoned, for some motive as yet unknown to us, then the possibility exists that the murderer will strike again.'

'He or she,' McIntosh reminded him, 'especially as the first place you'll need to look is in the victim's family circle.' He shrugged. 'Devoted family like that too.'

Faro regarded him cynically. The words were beginning to have a familiarly hollow ring. As for his superior, McIntosh could display almost childlike credulity at times, quite at odds with a tough exterior and more than thirty years' experience of violent crimes and criminals.

His own thoughts at that moment were concentrated not only on who had given Cedric Langweil an overdose of arsenic, but also on why? To kill a man known to be dying imminently called for an exceptional motive. If he could find it, then he was half-way to success.

His compassion lay with the murdered man's daughter Grace and the inevitable repercussions on her relationship with Vince when his detective stepfather metaphorically tightened the noose around the neck of one of her so-called 'devoted family'.

Walking slowly homeward through the moonlight, the cold and pitiless beauty of a frosty evening with the stars bright above Salisbury Crags, Faro thought sadly how so much beauty wears a mask of cruelty. And he remembered his own thoughts of a week ago, how he had been congratulating himself on how well their lives were going.

'Tempting the gods,' he said out loud. 'I should have known better.' That's what always happens. Measure happiness, feel secure, and it all vanishes like fairy gold.

His next call must be upon Cedric's widow, Maud. Fully aware of the nature of questions to be asked, such poking and prying into her distressed and shocked condition filled him with a natural disgust.

Could he take the coward's way out and ask if the enquiry could be delegated to someone else? He was sorely tempted. Knowing Vince's personal involvement with the Langweils, McIntosh would understand.

The more he thought of it the greater temptation became, but even more clearly came realization that he could not abandon Vince and the Langweils. The fact that his stepson was involved made it even more imperative that he personally solve the case. He could not take a chance on some other less experienced detective, working on a case where the evidence of one suspect was so inviting, reaching a false and fatal conclusion.

Distasteful as it was, he had no alternative but to proceed along the given lines. He needed a helper, someone strong, steady, and reliable, and the face of Danny

McQuinn passed uneasily before his eyes. Once his old enemy, Sergeant McQuinn had recently returned enriched by his experience working with the Glasgow City Police. Whatever his personal feelings, Faro knew McQuinn would be a good man to have at his side.

Although his methods were a little too ruthless and tactless for the genteel drawing rooms of middle-class Edinburgh, McQuinn's easy manner and common touch was particularly expert in extracting confidences from the servants' hall. He had a natural charm with the female sex, which Faro had secretly envied when on more than one occasion such information had helped to solve a baffling case.

Black haired, blue eyed, with an abundance of Irish charm and good looks, the sergeant listened intently when Faro put the facts of the case before him. 'Superintendent McIntosh wants this conducted with the utmost discretion.'

'You can rely on me for that, sir. I suggest the kitchens at Priorsfield would be a good place to begin.'

As they parted, McQuinn saluted him gravely and then with a cheeky grin. 'Good to work with you again, sir. You'll be pleased to know that Glasgow has sharpened my wits.'

Not that they needed much sharpening, was the rejoinder Faro might have made in the past but now bit back in the interests of diplomacy.

Before leaving the Central Office, he learned that arson was now added to the perplexing fraud case near Musselburgh. He set off on the train once more, deciding that if the poisoner of Cedric Langweil lurked, as he suspected, within the family circle, it did no harm to allow a couple of days for the shock of possible exposure to take its toll of already frayed nerves.

As the train carried him towards his destination Faro considered the motives of his two chief suspects in the Langweil case. Theodore, who had shared the last bottle of wine with Cedric, and could so easily have tampered

47

with the final glass. Was there some information about the family business that had decided him to speed on his brother's end, before new documents could be drawn up or an existing will revised?

Then there was Adrian, Vince's friend and partner. Adrian, who had personally dispensed the powder for his brother's indigestion.

Perhaps Adrian had the best motive of all. Inheritance. Cedric's death drew him one step nearer the Langweil fortune. Yet that didn't make sense either, if he believed that his elder brother was doomed anyway.

Of the two, Faro favoured Theodore. And he knew the reason why. Barbara. But even if she were free, did goddesses ever marry policemen?

Turning his thoughts away from such folly he was conscious of something at the back of his mind which was of vital importance. A shadowy something he had seen, or heard, that suggested he might, unlike this train, be on the wrong track completely when on Monday morning those other wheels of the law went into motion.

The opening of the official enquiry, police interviews with the Langweils, and the inevitable unpleasantness of muddied waters vigorously stirred, signalled the investigation he knew he had least wanted in his whole career.

Before that the weekend lay before him, two whole days with his daughter Rose, a small oasis in a desert of despair.

Chapter Five

Faro watched while the Orkney boat docked at Leith, his spirits downcast by the icy wind blowing across the River Forth.

Vince and Grace had insisted on accompanying him. Leaving them in the carriage, both pretending that nothing in their lives had changed, he wished more than ever that he could have delayed or postponed Rose's arrival.

He had an ominous feeling whatever the outcome of the official enquiry into the circumstances of Cedric's death this domestic tragedy must inevitably touch and indeed even engulf his own household.

His mind was so absorbed by his misgivings that he failed to recognize immediately the young woman who was waving to him so frantically from the boat rail.

It took him several seconds to realize that this was his daughter Rose. A new Rose in a fashionable blue velvet cape and bonnet. As she ran lightly down the gangway and he clasped her in his arms, he realized that his little lass had vanished for ever.

Their embrace told him that this Rose was already rounded in early womanhood. It came as a considerable shock that the six months that had elapsed since their last meeting could have brought about such changes, giving much and, alas, taking much away.

As she kissed him, and clinging to his arm hurried towards the waiting carriage, he had only time to warn her that Grace had lost her father before the two leaped from the carriage to greet them.

And now Faro saw his own astonishment mirrored in Vince's eyes. Having hugged her stepbrother, Rose was shyly greeting Grace. Watching the two girls, Faro and Vince exchanged glances, delight on Vince's face, bewilderment, even a little resentment on Faro's, for to the casual observer, Rose, well rounded, and Grace, slightly built, seemed little different in age.

And Faro saw too with a pang of loss that Rose was going to be as curvaceous and bonny as her mother his dear Lizzie had been, except that she was taller, and her resemblance to Vince, the same blond curls and bright eyes, was steadily increasing with the years.

As they headed for Sheridan Place, Rose spoke gently to Grace, offering her condolences. Grace's eyes filled with tears while Vince and Faro too felt the echoes of that anguish, the full depths of the tragedy which had robbed her of a beloved papa and had stricken that happy carefree family to the heart.

Grace looked across at Vince and said sadly, 'Our wedding, alas, has had to be postponed.'

But Grace was too sensible and practical a young person to let her own deep sorrow cloud over Rose's arrival in Edinburgh. Straightening her shoulders, she dabbed at her eyes and tried a brave smile. 'You know, of course, that I was once a pupil at the Grange Academy for Young Ladies. In fact, it was on my recommendation that Vince chose it for you. They have an excellent reputation in the department of foreign languages.'

She spoke enthusiastically about the teachers and the rules. But like all schoolgirls, it was the uniform that concerned Rose most of all. 'Is it becoming?' she asked anxiously.

'My dear, I would never have recommended it otherwise.'

Rose smiled gratefully at Vince. But such trivialities had not been the reason for his choice. Certain that marriage into the Langweil family would open up all manner of splendid matrimonial chances for his pretty stepsister, Vince felt the acquisition of a little extra culture and learning would not come amiss in the circles in which they would move.

Rose's reasons were quite different, her ambitions more modest than those of her stepbrother. Her heart long set on becoming a governess, she fancied this was the way for a young lady to enjoy foreign travel. And the acquisition of French and German would be to her advantage.

'The Queen has made Scotch governesses very popular among European royalty,' said Grace encouragingly. 'Especially when so many of them are related to her. And we have lots of very distinguished contacts in foreign embassies, have we not, Vince?'

Grace smiling, tried to include him in the conversation, while Rose listened wide-eyed to the prospects opening before her.

When at last Rose and her father were deposited at Sheridan Place, Grace declined the invitation to join them for tea.

'I do not care to leave Mama on her own just at present,' she said apologetically. 'But very soon you shall come to tea with your father and I will take you to all the best shops in Princes Street.'

Delighted with such a promise, hugs were exchanged under the approving eye of Vince. Then the door of 9 Sheridan Place opened and Rose was delivered into the welcoming arms of the housekeeper Mrs Brook. Her 'bairn' was home again.

'Let me look at you, Miss Rose. My, you are a young lady now. How you've grown. I'd never have recognized you, not even if we had passed one another in Princes Street. Isn't she lovely. Inspector? Aren't you proud of your little girl. And you, Dr Vince, what have you to say?'

The two men murmured the replies expected of them as Rose, sparkling-eyed, was swept upstairs to her room by Mrs Brook. 'Now tell me all about Miss Emily—'

As they sat down to dinner that evening, Faro too wished

51

for news of his younger daughter, feeling guilty that she had not accompanied her sister.

Rose shook her head. 'Emily does not mind in the least. She is happy and content in Kirkwall. She is clever with her hands, not like me, she thrives on cold winds and stormy days,' she added with a shudder. 'Edinburgh frightens little Emily, Papa. She loathes sea voyages and besides, she says she would hate to live in a great city. I think she will be quite content to settle down with an Orkney farmer some day. And she shouldn't have much trouble finding a husband. Already the young men have an eye on her, much to Grandmama's distress.'

Leaning across the table, she smiled at him. 'We aren't a bit alike really. I take after you, Papa. You've always said that. And now I see it's true. I'm eternally curious, I want to know everything about everything . . .'

Faro was inordinately proud of Rose, as they walked arm in arm along the Princes Street Gardens after church on Sunday, aware of admiring glances in her direction and delighted to introduce her to several acquaintances who were more ardent churchgoers than himself.

Conscious that religion played a very small part in his own life, Faro felt that like marriage it seemed too complicated for a policeman to handle successfully. But shy of admitting such a fact to his daughter, he had accompanied her to St Giles where – it seemed only a few years ago – she had been christened.

Walking in the warm sunshine, his present anxieties about the Langweils retreated to a safe distance, banished by Rose's enthusiasm. Her energy limitless, she insisted on visiting all her favourite places again.

Calton Hill, the Castle, and Holyrood Park. From the top of Arthur's Seat they looked on Edinburgh spread out before them, the distant prospect of the Bass Rock, the East Lothian coastline.

Rose clapped her hands excitedly. 'Well, Papa, where now?'

'No more, I beg you.' Faro groaned. 'Unless you want to carry your poor father home.'

The promise of afternoon tea, with scones and cakes delectably prepared by Mrs Brook, was all the temptation a healthy young appetite needed.

As they ate together, and laughed and reminisced, he realized that his brief sojourn in the happy world of domesticity was almost over. Tomorrow loomed unpleasantly near. And tomorrow he would be Detective Inspector Faro again, with all that implied.

When, early on Monday morning, Faro entered Charlotte Square and walked up the front steps of the Langweil town house to talk to Cedric's widow, he was in time to encounter Dr Wiseman taking his departure.

The doctor greeted him nervously, eyeing him with some suspicion.

'I trust you are not here in an official capacity, Inspector. My patients are understandably shocked and upset.'

'Quite so, Doctor. This is just a routine matter.'

As he walked away, the doctor turned. 'For your information, Inspector, I cannot think of any reason why Cedric Langweil should have pretended to be seriously ill. He would never have needlessly distressed his family. Or anyone else. He was a kind father and husband.'

'Then who told him that he was a dying man? He must have consulted someone?'

'I haven't the least idea who he consulted. Except that it wasn't myself. You are the detective, sir. Perhaps if you could find the missing doctor, you might get more results than plaguing his unfortunate family.'

'I appreciate your sentiments, Doctor, but I am not conducting this enquiry for my own pleasure. My stepson and Miss Langweil are shortly to be married. They – and I – are intimately concerned in the outcome of this enquiry. I assure you we are all distressed by this unhappy turn of events—'

'Is that so?' Wiseman interrupted sharply. 'Then all I can say is that Dr Laurie might have handled the whole affair with more discretion.'

'By discretion, am I to presume you mean ignoring the obvious?'

Dr Wiseman smiled bitterly. 'I can assure you, Inspector, that what you call the obvious has been done by many in the medical profession before today, and I dare say will be done often again, and for no more sinister purpose than to spare the family.'

'Suppressing dangerous evidence, Doctor. Is that what you are implying?'

Wiseman shrugged. 'Surely it is not outwith the bounds of possibility even for you to imagine that a man who feared he was gravely ill might decide to take his own life.'

'Except that by suicide his family would forfeit any insurance claim.'

'I doubt that the matter of an insurance made forfeit would weigh very heavily upon the fortunes of the Langweils. As for Mrs Cedric Langweil, it is no secret that she is very well connected.'

Pausing to let that information sink in, he said: 'And I understand that Miss Langweil inherits a comfortable income on her twenty-first birthday. By which time she will be the wife of Dr Laurie. All going well in that direction, of course,' he added significantly. 'Good day to you, sir.'

For a physician who rarely attended the Langweils, Wiseman was particularly well informed about his patients' prospects, Faro thought as he waited in the extravagantly furnished hall with its marble statues, staircase, and lofty cupola.

Town houses in an expanding Edinburgh were no longer a necessity for the rich. With better roads Priorsfield House was easily accessible; the long and tortuous coach journey to Duddingston, liable to be snowbound in winter, was a distant memory. Considering the size of Priorsfield a separate establishment for the younger brother seemed excessive, especially at a time when all over Edinburgh less fortunate families shared one bedroom and the poor of the High Street tenements lived out their lives in one room.

Doubtless Cedric had his own reasons for not wishing to reside in one vast wing of the family home.

'Perhaps the reason that they have a close business relationship makes living apart desirable. Or possibly their wives wish to be independent,' Vince had told him. 'Grace tells me that her parents moved into Charlotte Square soon after Theodore remarried. Now don't you feel that is significant? The young wife with new young ideas. I fear Maud is a little conventional, rather rigid in her outlook.'

Alerted by footsteps above, it was Grace Langweil who stared down at him from the upper floor. Running lightly down the stairs to greet him, he fancied that she kissed his cheek with less enthusiasm than she had done hitherto.

'I was expecting Rose to be with you. I hoped to take her shopping with me. I presume it is Mama you wish to see.'

Faro was aware of a coolness about his future step-daughter-in-law that he regarded ominously. He had hoped that the pleasant interlude of Rose's arrival had put them back on their former easy footing. However, her manner said plainer than any words that he was already regarded as the one to blame, the instigator of the reign of terror her father's unfortunate demise had inflicted upon the family.

'Rose was still abed when I left the house. She will be arriving later.' And taking her hands in a determined manner, he asked: 'And how are you this morning, my dear?'

'None of us is sleeping well. That's hardly to be wondered at.' Her reply and slight withdrawal from him indicated that asking after her health was lacking in tact and sensitivity.

'You will need to return later if you wish to see Mama. Dr Wiseman has prescribed a sedative. You must realize how terribly upset she is, by all this – this business,' she added reproachfully. 'Bad enough for her knowing how ill dear Papa was for months, without these ridiculous suggestions that he has been poisoned.'

Faro laid a hand on her arm. She was trembling. 'Grace, my dear, you must believe me, I feel deeply for you in all this. And Vince too, but the law must proceed whatever our personal feelings. And the law calls for an enquiry in such circumstances.'

'Surely with all your influence you could have spared us—' she began hotly.

'That I cannot do, much as I would wish to out of regard for your family, not if there is any possibility, however great or small, that death did not come about by natural causes.'

'Oh, this is intolerable,' she cut in. 'You mean you really do believe that someone in Priorsfield poisoned dear Papa. One of our servants, perhaps. If you knew how devoted they were to him. The idea is so preposterous, only a policeman who did not know us could give that a second thought.'

Faro winced from the contempt in her voice, the anger in her gaze, but he said gently as he could, 'My dear, I have had second, third, and even fourth thoughts, believe me. Murder is an endless chain, once established with a link, it has an unhappy tendency to lead on and on—'

'Murder? In this family? You must be mad – or entirely wicked – to even imagine such a thing. If it wasn't so terrible, it would be laughable.'

Her face pink with anger, Faro regarded her with compassion. Poor innocent child, how would she ever cope with the even more monstrous truth: that the most probable explanation to which the scanty evidence thus far pointed was that for some reason as yet unknown, her father had been murdered not by a servant but by one of his, and her, close kin.

'You must believe me, my dear, what I am hoping to prove is not who is guilty but who isn't.'

What else could he say? But his words had the required effect and Grace, mollified, shrugged.

'Very well. You can start with me. I adored my father. I have absolutely no motive for wishing him – him—' Her voice broke. 'Dead. I had not the slightest notion that he was dying. He had bouts of indigestion and suffered from bad headaches. And I used to, God help me, tease him, about drinking too much port. Tease him about – getting old. Oh – Oh.'

And sobbing she steadied herself against the staircase and Faro took her into his arms, held her against his shoulder.

'There, there, my dear. There, there.'

Suddenly he was aware of Maud Langweil's face regarding them from the top landing. Slowly she descended the stairs, holding firmly to the banister. Deep mourning's black bombazine and flowing crêpe did not become her, its dramatic veils enveloped her, making a pale face and lips paler, light eyes lighter. It drained every shred of living colour from her countenance.

She took Grace from him. 'There, my darling, hush now. Don't distress yourself.'

'Mama, you should be resting. Remember what Dr Wiseman said,' she added with a reproachful look at Faro.

'I'm quite rested, darling. I gather Mr Faro is here to see me. We will talk in the sitting room.'

Grace regarded her mother's face anxiously. 'Are you sure, Mama?'

'Of course I'm sure. No, I don't need you, dearest. Go to the kitchen and get Molly to give you a nice soothing drink. Now, off you go, there's a good girl.'

As he followed her upstairs, she said: 'I am looking forward very much to meeting Rose. Grace tells me she is absolutely charming. I am sure they will be great friends. After all there is little difference in their ages – or so it seems to those of us who are middle aged.'

In the sitting room, the door firmly closed, Maud said, 'Please be seated, Mr Faro. I am most anxious to give you all the help I can to clear up this unfortunate misunderstanding regarding my late husband. I do realize that this is no ordinary enquiry for you either, and it is as painful and as difficult for you as for any of the family. As you know Vince is already like a son to me, the son I never had.'

She paused to smile at him sadly. 'That I gather we have in common, for you also lost a son long ago. You must try not to think of us now as your enemies, your suspects, Mr Faro. We are indeed your friends and

Vince's. And if my late husband did not die from the disease we believed was killing him, then we are as eager to co-operate with the law and find whatever, or whoever, ended his life.'

Up to now Maud had made no impression upon him. At their few meetings, she had seemed something of a nonentity among the bright and shining Langweils. Obedient to her husband's commands in public, the dutiful hostess, the devoted mother but with little conversation that was not merely a yes or no, an echo of her spouse's sentiments. A woman not encouraged to suffer original thoughts or express opinions of her own.

Now he looked at her with new admiration. This was not the widow he had dreaded meeting, devastated, distraught, eternally weeping. Maud Langweil it seemed was one of those admirable women dismissed as frail, spoilt by a lifetime of riches, that men expect to collapse under adversity and are constantly surprised, as he was, that instead they find new fortitude in facing up to life's tragedies.

'Will you take tea with me?'

Faro noticed that the tea tray had already been in service and presumably Doctor Wiseman had accepted the invitation he now declined. If Mrs Langweil could have read his thoughts and his expression, she would have realized at that moment he would have greeted with enthusiasm something considerably stronger than the China tea on offer.

'Very well.' Maud sat in the high-backed chair, her face in shadow. 'What can I tell you, Mr Faro, that would be of help to you? I understand you believe my late husband was poisoned.'

Chapter Six

Faro was taken aback by her directness. He suspected that she was mistress of the situation despite Grace's claim that her mother was too distressed to talk to him. He was also embarrassed, at a loss for the appropriate response. The kind of questions he was used to asking widows, whose husbands had died under very suspicious circumstances and arsenic poisoning, were suddenly quite shocking before this gentle woman whose daughter was to marry his stepson.

And yet – and yet. In the past had he not conducted just such interviews in just such elegant surroundings with an apparently inconsolable heart-broken widow? Invariably a young widow in the course of investigation revealed as a scheming murderess who had heartlessly watched an old husband die a slow and agonizing death. To gain a fortune, or an insurance, or to free her for a waiting lover's fond embrace.

Barbara's face loomed before him in all its unattainable loveliness. The sudden thought appalled him.

Could there possibly have been a ghastly mistake? Had it been Theodore and not Cedric who was the intended victim?

Observing Maud Langweil closely as she attended to the tea ritual, her hands were quite steady, and Faro would have found it difficult to doubt that he was regarding an innocent woman.

He prided himself upon occasional flashes of intuition and decided he would be surprised indeed to discover that Cedric's widow had secret reasons for wishing to rid herself of an unwanted husband. The whole idea seemed ludicrous, even indecent, to contemplate, especially as she was so eager to befriend his daughter.

Again he wished he had been able to postpone Rose's arrival for enrolment at the Academy. The thought of his daughter besmirched by association with the as yet undiscovered murderer in the Langweil household was sickening, intolerable.

As if interpreting his discomfiture, Maud asked: 'I suppose the question that is framing itself in your mind and that you are too polite to ask is the obvious one: Were the relations between my late husband and myself quite amicable?'

Her casual tone took him aback, especially as she paused with the teacup half-way to her lips and said: 'Isn't that what you really are here to find out? If we were happy together?'

Faro took a deep breath: 'And were you?'

'Indeed we were. The best of friends and comrades as well as having a marriage as harmonious as most of our friends' after twenty years.'

When Faro frowned, she again interpreted his thoughts. 'Perhaps that answers the next question you are too much of a gentleman, outside your professional capacity, to ask: Did Cedric have a mistress?'

Looking towards the window, she smiled as if at a sudden vision. 'He may in the way of many gentlemen who belong to private clubs and societies have had access to ladies of a certain profession.' Her shrug was eloquent. 'I never enquired, nor had I any desire to know of such occasions. A man is a man, Mr Faro, and we women are brought up to realize that such small indiscretions are part of their nature but have naught to do with destroying the structure of an otherwise happy marriage.'

She shrugged. 'We are taught to tolerate such matters and ignore them. Lusts of the moment and nothing more, Mr Faro. With as little lasting effect as the gratification of appetite. Which in fact, as a man, you must recognize is all that it is—'

Faro was saved the further embarrassment of a reply to this forthright condemnation of his sex's morals by a tap at the door.

'Mama?' Grace looked in anxiously. 'Are you able to see Madame Rich? Or shall I ask her to come back later?'

'No, my dear. Tell her I will see her. If Mr Faro will excuse us. Madame Rich is our dressmaker,' she explained. 'We have certain requirements for mourning attire – and orders that must now be postponed for Grace's spring wedding,' she added with a small sigh.

Faro held open the door for her, and she turned to him anxiously. 'I do apologize, Mr Faro, for I have not answered all of your questions.'

As they descended the stairs, she added: 'Do please come again if you think I can help you in any way.'

At the front door, she extended her hand. 'I can only assure you of one thing. That my husband loved me, and his daughter. A good father and husband, a splendid employer – everyone who met him and knew him will tell you that. I can think of no earthly reason why anyone should wish to murder him. Certainly not in this household.'

Since the time of Cedric's death pointed to the fatal dose of arsenic having been administered in Priorsfield, Faro was thankful that he did not have to interview the servants.

Walking briskly down Princes Street in the direction of the High Street and the Central Office, he heard rapid footsteps behind him.

It was Sergeant Danny McQuinn. 'Been interviewing the sorrowing widow, sir?'

McQuinn's words made Faro wince. Words that were all too often used mockingly in the Edinburgh City Police.

'I was in the servants' hall. Heard you leaving.'

'You didn't waste much time. Anything to report?'

McQuinn shook his head. 'Think she's guilty?' he asked eagerly. 'Tricky situation for you, sir, going to be a relative by marriage and so forth. No doubt you have a reluctance – '

Faro ceased walking and regarded the young sergeant sternly. 'I have no reluctance, McQuinn. If she damned well poisoned her husband then she's as guilty as any common murderer. And she'll suffer the same fate if I can prove it,' he added angrily, and proceeded to walk faster than ever.

'Your stepson's future mother-in-law, Inspector?' McQuinn's long stride kept an easy pace with him. 'Now that would create a sensation in the police, wouldn't it now?'

McQuinn laughed, then, perhaps taking pity on Faro's agonized expression, said: 'But you don't really think she's guilty, do you? Nice lady like that. If it consoles you, no one below stairs would believe it either. They think the world of her. And of the master, as they call him.'

'What else did you find out?'

McQuinn sighed. 'Not a lot, sir. On this visit, I thought it tactful to take refuge in a little subterfuge.'

'What kind of subterfuge?'

'Lies, Inspector,' McQuinn said cheerfully. 'But like all the best distortions of fact, based on a core of truth. As you know there are always burglaries in this area. Not too difficult to invent a cache of objects found near their basement. Worked a treat. All the maids were suitably impressed. No, there was nothing missing of that description from their establishment.'

Again McQuinn laughed. 'And I would have been the most surprised man on earth if there had been. However, there wasn't much point in prolonging the visit seeing it was Priorsfield where their master died.'

And taking out the handsome silver timepiece which McQuinn proudly boasted was 'a parting gift from my Glasgow colleagues', he added: 'Looks as if I have just enough time to present the robbery story to the servants there. With a bit of luck, I'll have more vital information from them. In fact, if I look sharpish, the Musselburgh train passes the gates.'

'Papa! Over here.'

Faro turned and there was Rose clutching her bonnet

against the shrill wind blowing up the Waverley Steps, and thereby affording, in her descent from the horse-drawn omnibus, a glimpse of slender ankles.

One look at McQuinn's amused face told Faro that he was suitably impressed by this revelation as breathlessly Rose rushed to her father's side.

'I am meeting Grace.' And smiling at McQuinn, she held out her hand. 'Hello.'

'Aren't you going to introduce me, sir?' said McQuinn, smiling delightedly.

'Introduce yourself,' laughed Rose. 'We are old friends.'

'We are?' McQuinn, plainly embarrassed, looked quickly at Faro and then to Rose and back again.

'Don't you remember? You once rescued me from probable death or dishonour when a silly French maid had mislaid me on the way from the Castle. Emily and I never did discover whether we were about to be abducted,' she added with a shiver. 'And Grandmama had wicked thoughts about white slavers.'

Gradual enlightenment dawned on McQuinn. 'But you were – I mean, it was two little girls I found wandering—'

'It was also years ago, when Papa was investigating the case of the baby in the wall of Edinburgh Castle.'

'By all that's holy, Miss Faro,' said McQuinn. 'Sure and who would have thought you'd grow into such a blithe and bonny young lady.'

As Rose blushed under McQuinn's appraising gaze Faro decided this had gone far enough. Hailing a passing hiring carriage, he bundled Rose into it with directions to Charlotte Square.

'But, Papa,' Rose protested. 'I can walk there. This is nonsense.'

'It isn't nonsense. And I won't have you walking about Princes Street, a stranger unescorted.'

'But – Papa—'

'Do as you're told,' said Faro, nodding to the driver and slipping him a coin. 'Now, off you go.'

Watching them depart, he said coldly to McQuinn:

'Haven't you a train to catch?' And without waiting for a reply, he hurried across the road and over North Bridge, murmuring angrily to himself that the last thing he wanted in his life at the present time was a daughter who was going to need watching.

Rose was already abed asleep when he returned to Sheridan Place late that evening and found a very gloomy Vince awaiting him.

'We've drawn a complete blank. Adrian and I have spoken to all the leading consultants in Edinburgh whom Cedric might have visited. Wiseman put in an appearance at the surgery, by the way, most anxious to help us. He'd met you at Charlotte Square and was baffled and rather hurt too, I might add. Feels that as a long-standing friend of the family, Adrian and Cedric should have confided in him and not gone above his head to consult another doctor.'

Vince looked at him. 'I was going to suggest that you cross Adrian off your list of suspects, then something happened to change my mind.'

'And what was that?' Faro demanded eagerly.

'As you know he's a good friend of mine and I thought I was in his confidence. However, Wiseman let slip an important piece of information during his visit. Freda came into the hall as he was leaving and he said: "I believe we are to congratulate you, Mrs Langweil." Freda blushed and smiled shyly. "I hope so." Then Wiseman said: "I trust your husband is taking good care of you. After all this long time, we don't want any problems, do we?"

'Well, there wasn't any doubt in my mind what he was talking about. Freda was pregnant. I'd noticed that she had put on rather a lot of weight recently, but fool that I was and because Adrian never said a word, its possible significance escaped me.

'When Adrian and I were alone, I added my own congratulations. He apologized for not telling me earlier and added somewhat hastily that as he hadn't told any of the family yet he would be grateful if I'd keep it to myself.

Early days still, and as they'd had a few false alarms. They intended telling the family at Barbara's birthday party next week.'

Both men were silent, aware that if Adrian and Freda produced a son, he would inherit the Langweil fortune after Theodore's death. Only Cedric had stood in the way. And now Cedric was dead.

'So only Adrian and Wiseman knew. You say Wiseman is a long-standing friend of the family?'

'Oh yes. I rather guess from Adrian that the main attraction was Grace. Adrian suspected that he had hopes of her, even teased him a little about it.'

'Surely she was a little young for him.'

'Not really, although she must have been a mere schoolgirl when he first went to the house.'

I must be getting old, thought Faro. But doubtless that was why Wiseman seemed so embarrassed and discomforted by his presence. Knowing that Faro's stepson was to marry Grace, he was afraid that the Inspector might be aware of his infatuation for his young patient and that his behaviour towards her was under constant scrutiny, the subject of mocking comment.

Faro could sympathize, since he was self-conscious as a guilty schoolboy in Barbara Langweil's presence, certain everyone guessed his feelings for her.

'I presume Grace never gave him any encouragement.'

Vince laughed. 'She regards him as a benevolent uncle. That he had any amorous inclinations had never occurred to her, I can assure you.'

Realizing they were slipping away from the vital subject once again, Faro said: 'As you've drawn a blank in Edinburgh with consultant physicians, I wonder if Cedric went elsewhere.'

'I suppose it's a possibility, Stepfather, but rather like searching for a needle in a haystack. You're thinking of London – somewhere like that?'

Vince frowned. 'I seem to remember he went to Aberdeen rather a lot. Something to do with the whisky business.'

'Then that is perhaps where we will find our missing consultant.'

'I'll put it to Adrian. See if he comes up with any names.'

'We have to clear this up, lad, make absolutely certain that he was not a dying man, before we can proceed with the possible enquiry into a murder.'

'My poor Grace,' whispered Vince with some feeling.

To which his stepfather added silently, my poor Vince. For whatever happened, if Inspector Faro succeeded in tracking down whoever poisoned Cedric Langweil, his triumph would shake the entire family to its very foundations and shatter the delicate fabric of Vince's forthcoming marriage to Grace Langweil.

Chapter Seven

'Vince has been called away to attend a sick child,' Rose told her father when they met at breakfast.

Faro was never at his best in the morning, especially when a murder case kept him awake half the night wrestling with theories, sifting through evidence, and discarding improbabilities. Since he was emotionally concerned with Cedric's death and the outcome, he had fallen into a deep and exhausted sleep at dawn.

Normally he always claimed he needed his first breaths of fresh air to sharpen his wits. Vince appreciated his stepfather's approach to each new morning and the two men were normally silent as each read his own mail and their comments were few and only where strictly necessary.

Rose, who saw her father rarely, was unaware that at breakfast time he was apt to be grumpy. She prattled at a great rate about her plans for the day. Grace was taking her to the shop where she could look at the school uniform and then they were to go on to the Botanic Gardens.

Faro listened, polite but vague and trying to smile a little, just to please her.

'You will enjoy that. I presume Grace will be calling for you in their carriage.'

Rose frowned. 'It is rather out of her way, Papa. I thought I would take the omnibus to Charlotte Square.' And clasping her hands delightedly, 'I do so enjoy public transport. We have nothing like that at home. It is quite thrilling—'

'Rose,' he interrupted. 'I must insist that you avail

yourself of Grace's carriage, or if you wish to explore, then you take Mrs Brook with you.'

'Mrs Brook—'

'Yes, my dear. You see, it isn't quite right for a young girl who is a stranger to Edinburgh to wander round unescorted.'

'How am I to cease being a stranger if I can't search out places for myself? I like my own company. Besides, I am used to going about Kirkwall alone.'

'Kirkwall is not Edinburgh. There are dangers in a city that you would not encounter in Orkney.'

'I'm not a child any longer, Papa,' Rose said in wounded tones.

'I am quite aware of that,' he said coldly.

Then, her heightened colour warning him that she was upset by his remark, he put his arm around her, hugged her to him.

'I want you to be happy here, my precious. And safe. I realize your old papa is a great fusspot, but do bear with me. Will you – please?'

Resting her head against his shoulder, her sunny smile restored, she said: 'Of course I will, dear Papa. I just love Edinburgh so much. I can hardly believe that I am to stay here soon – for always – with you. And I want to know everything about it.'

'And so you shall, love. Now – another piece of toast?'

Fondly he watched her pour out his second cup of tea. She was so lovely, this daughter of his. It was a dream come true, having her sit there across the table. They would soon get used to each other's ways.

As he was leaving for the Central Office, she helped him into his cape and, handing him his hat, smiled.

'Aren't you fortunate to have Sergeant McQuinn with you. Such a nice man, isn't he? He'll look well after you, I'm sure.'

Faro bit back an angry response at thus being entrusted to his sergeant's care, kissed her goodbye, and with the domestic harmony only slightly dinted by her innocent remarks walked more sharply than usual in the direction of the High Street and the Central Office.

There McQuinn awaited him, busily writing notes at his desk.

'Well, sir, I've been to Priorsfield. Mention of burglars in the district works wonders,' he added with a chuckle. 'I sternly demanded what security measures they had on hand and as one thing led to another I expressed an admiration for all those lovely exotic potted plants and was told they came from Mr Theodore's greenhouses.

' "How do you keep them so well?" I asked. "I hope if any of you are using poisonous chemicals you sign for them."

'And what did I discover? That the only poison used in that house was rat poison.'

'Rat poison?'

'Rat poison, the very same, Inspector. Arsenic, ordered and signed for by who but Mr Cedric himself.'

'Don't you mean Mr Theodore?'

'No, definitely Cedric. Like you I thought they had said the wrong name. But it seems that most of the Langweil business is conducted from Priorsfield. According to Mrs Gimmond, there were rats in all their malthouses. Everyone knew about that, but Mr Theodore also left domestic matters like vermin extermination to his brother.

'As you know there's been a plague of rats in the sewers for as long as folk can remember. In spite of all attempts to get rid of them, no sooner is one old rat-infested building pulled down than they spread like wildfire into the foundations of the other houses.'

Faro nodded. 'Including Priorsfield, McQuinn,' as he remembered Piers Strong's argument for hygiene, for an all-clean, rat-free Edinburgh. 'They're an infernal nuisance.'

'Right, sir. And I gather Mr Theodore wasn't aware of their presence until he found they had gnawed their way into his new library. Carried in with boxes of old books stored in the cellars they were nesting behind the shelving.

'The maids all shuddered and squealed going on about how they went to light fires in the morning they could hear the rats scuttling about.'

'So there was arsenic in the house.'

'A plentiful supply, to all accounts. And in regular use,' was the reply.

'Did you get the impression that Cedric had any enemies on the staff?'

'No. From what Mrs Gimmond said, he was well liked. Seemed she was acquainted with the servants in Charlotte Square too. Said they were all shocked, that he had been a good master and would be sadly missed.' McQuinn frowned and shook his head. 'But you know, I got an odd impression that she didn't care for him personally.'

'Indeed? How so?'

McQuinn frowned. 'Nothing in what she said, but her face gave it away somehow.'

'What is she like, this Mrs Gimmond?'

'Handsome woman. Well spoken. Not quite the wife you'd expect Gimmond the butler to have. Odd that she'd marry a low-class chap like him.'

Faro looked at McQuinn. Gimmond's impeccable accent hadn't fooled his sergeant. 'What makes you think he's low class?' he asked.

McQuinn shrugged. 'You can always tell. Something in his manner gives him away. He's not quite the ticket, not confident enough. I've met a lot of butlers in my time and Gimmond is not quite easy in the part.' He shook his head. 'You know, sir, I wouldn't be at all surprised if he's had trouble with the police at some time. He has that nervousness, the sidelong shifty look that old lags display when a uniform shows up on the doorstep and their old sins begin to bother them.'

Faro remained silent. He was not at that moment prepared to take McQuinn into his confidence about Gimmond's past. But his sergeant's observations were worth noting.

'Did you get any useful information about upstairs?'

'Scandal, you mean?' grinned McQuinn. 'Not a whiff. As I said, all seemed to be blessed harmony, a devoted family. Not only working together but holidays too. Never seemed to tire of each other's company. As you know, I expect, the brothers were also keen golfers and their wives often accompanied them. That seemed to surprise Mrs Gimmond. Quite unusual for keen golfers to want their wives along, she said.'

Faro smiled. 'You've done very well, McQuinn.'

McQuinn laughed. 'And I've been invited to look in again. So I'll keep at it. Mrs Gimmond is a good cook too.'

'I would have expected that.'

'But then, Inspector, you're not a poor bachelor like me. You have good connections.'

Faro refused to rise to the bait even when McQuinn added with a grin: 'How's that pretty daughter of yours, sir? Staying long?'

'She is here to finish her education. Going to school.'

McQuinn whistled. 'School, is it? Well, well, you astonish me. I'd have thought she was more ready to be here to find a husband,' he added with a grin.

Faro seized the papers on his desk without further comment. He was determined to stick to his resolution to stay on cordial terms with McQuinn and not allow his sergeant's abrasive personality to threaten the efficient performance of their working relationship.

'Where next, Inspector?'

'Somehow, somewhere, we need to track down whoever attended Cedric Langweil and told him that he had a diseased brain which was going to kill him in six months.'

'Sounds like Dr Laurie's domain.'

It was, but all enquiries regarding the missing consultant seemed doomed to failure.

And then they had a piece of luck.

Faro found a note awaiting him from Maud Langweil. With it a letter of condolence from a Dr Henry Longfield who had just heard on his return from New York that Cedric had died.

'Perhaps he will be able to help you,' Maud wrote. 'He has been in America for the past six months. It is possible that Cedric saw him just before he left.'

When Vince read the letter, he looked almost happy for the first time in weeks. An enquiry at Surgeons' Hall confirmed that Longfield dealt with cancer patients at the Infirmary. He was also a consultant physician.

Considerably heartened by this information, Faro went to visit the doctor in his house in Moray Place.

Dr Longfield was not dismayed by the presence of a detective inspector. The police often called when sudden death required discreet enquiries.

'Cedric was a friend of mine, yes. We had known each other since student days and I was sorry to hear of his death.'

'Sorry but not surprised?'

The doctor frowned. 'Both, as it happened. Why do you ask?'

'Did he ever consult you professionally?'

'Only once, curiously enough, just before I left for America. He wanted me to give him a thorough examination. I did so and gave him a clean bill of health.'

'You mean there was no sign of illness?'

'None at all. He was strong and healthy, in excellent condition – a man in the prime of his life. It would not have surprised me had he lived to be ninety. And yet such things do happen. Massive heart attack, was it?'

'Not exactly. I will be frank with you, Doctor. Cedric Langweil's death is baffling. He told his family that he had a brain disease and was unlikely to live until the end of the year. Which prediction was in fact correct. But that was not how he died . . .'

And Faro proceeded to relate the facts as he knew them.

At the end, Longfield was silent for a moment. 'So that is the reason for this visit, Inspector. It does sound as if someone gave him a helping hand. Curious, because on several occasions he showed considerable interest in the workings of the human brain. Why we did certain things and so forth; a true Darwinian, he regarded man as just a little higher than the apes. Often he said it was only our superior thought processes that kept us above the

72

laws of the jungle. Some of us, that is,' he added with a wry smile.

'In fact, now that I give it particular thought in the light of what you have told me, Cedric frequently asked me what were the first indications of disease of the brain. Most unfortunate,' he sighed, 'this morbid preoccupation must have preyed on his mind until he believed that he was suffering from some abnormal condition.'

He shrugged sadly. 'The result was that he took his own life, in a state of mental aberration and disturbance. And yet that does amaze me. You see, he did not strike me as a man who would entertain such notions. He loved and lived life to the full even as a student. He would never accept the second best and he worshipped beauty.'

The picture of Cedric greedy for life did not fit the picture of the desperate man who believing he was dying, panicked, thought Faro as he thanked the doctor for his help.

Returning to the Central Office Faro realized that the interview he most dreaded could no longer be delayed or avoided.

He must talk to Barbara Langweil, who had also been present in Priorsfield when her brother-in-law died.

Faro was more than usually nervous about the procedure, anxious not to upset that beautiful sensitive woman by any hint that she was responsible for Cedric's unfortunate demise under her roof. Or since the evidence pointed to his having been murdered that her hand might have been capable of administering the fatal dose of arsenic.

Gathering together the notes that he had written on the case so far, Faro leaned back in his chair, his back rigid as he closed his eyes and his mind tightly against such a thought.

That his goddess might also be capable of murder.

73

Chapter Eight

Walking rapidly in the direction of Duddingston, Faro
was again aware of the historic drama of Scotland's past
surrounding him.

To his left the sun glanced off the rolling fields outlining
the parallel lines of the old runrig system of agriculture.
Begun with the monks and discontinued long ago, its
evidence was still visible also on the upper reaches of
Arthur's Seat, whose towering mass overhung the road
on which he walked.

Samson's Ribs, they called it. Out of sight lay Hunter's
Bog, where once the Young Pretender had camped with
his troops, certain of victory. Looming darkly on the
horizon above Duddingston Loch, Craigmillar Castle.
Within those now ruined and roofless walls the Prince's
thrice-great-grandmother Mary Queen of Scots had,
according to legend, let the besotted Earl of Bothwell
whisper in her ear a plan to rid a wife of a loathsomely
diseased and unwanted husband.

As Faro entered the iron gates of Priorsfield he was
again aware that an air of mysteries unsolved, lost in
time, clung to the great house before him. He would not
have admitted to his colleagues in the Central Office, or
to a great many other people, his belief that as well as
bricks and mortar houses were built of the lives of the
generations who have lived there, their memories of good
and evil, their scenes of sadness and joy absorbed into
the stones.

What then was the strand linking Prince Charles
Edward Stuart's fortunes with the humble alehouse that

had been Priorsfield? And the mystery never to be solved of French gold that might have changed the destiny of the Stuart monarchy? And what of the skeleton dug up a century later with a knife in its ribs?

Sometime he must talk to Grace about her ghost. Children were sensitive to such things and for his money, Priorsfield, secret in its nest of trees, seemed haunted by more than raucous crows.

Out of sight, the peacocks screeched a warning.

He shuddered. He didn't like peacocks, they offended his sense of justice that an unfeeling Creator had crippled such beauty by a terrible voice.

Gimmond opened the door to him. As usual they exchanged a minimum of words.

'I will see if the mistress can see you.'

Waiting in the hall, Faro rehearsed his opening speech to Barbara with such elaborate anxiety he decided it would be a relief if she were unable to see him.

He was almost surprised when Gimmond returned. 'Will you come this way, sir. Mrs Langweil will receive you in the library.'

Barbara was seated by the window, overlooking the drive. She must have seen his approach and as always, at that first glance, her beauty took him by the throat, rendered him speechless.

Unlike her sister-in-law, deep mourning became her, the veils and jet adding vulnerability, enhancing the luminosity of her skin, the brightness of her eyes. Where grief blotched other faces, eyes reddened, here was a woman who cried and became even more beautiful.

More desirable. His eyes avoided the slightly heaving bosom, the tiny hand-spanned waist. He tried to glance at her sternly, painfully aware of the honey-coloured hair, of amber eyes that changed colour. Her hands were very white, with long tapered fingers. Her handshake was lingering, cool.

She dismissed his apologetic, stammering reasons for 'this unexpected visit' with a smile.

'It is necessary, I quite understand. In the distressing

circumstances of my brother-in-law's death I realize you must interview all members of the family who were present in the house. You must do your duty, Inspector Faro, however unpleasant.'

Another smile, brilliant this time, revealed small exquisitely white teeth, lips very red against the ivory skin. 'Please go ahead, I am quite ready. I thought it was quite vital that you should see these, for instance.'

With the important air of a conjuror producing rabbits from a hat, she took from the side table cards on which were written the menus for that fatal evening's dinner party.

Faro was more interested in the list of the wines.

'Will they help in your enquiries?'

'A little.'

'How else can I assist you then? Please do not hesitate to ask – anything. And I will try to answer.'

She was very anxious to please, but the answers to his routine questions were valueless.

Did she know of any reason why someone should poison Cedric Langweil? No. Did he have any enemies? No.

And the more searching: 'Were the relations between your husband and his brother amicable?' And softening the blow, 'Any business troubles, perhaps?'

He thought that question brought a fleeting shadow, the merest hint of a frown. The instant later it was gone.

'I know of none. My husband told me you had asked him if Cedric had any enemies, if there was a family feud.'

She looked at him boldly. 'I can only confirm what he said to you, Mr Faro, add my assurance to his. You must believe us when we tell you that in this family we are all devoted to one another. And loyal too.'

Aye, and there's the rub, thought Faro. Loyal. That's the insurmountable barrier all policemen stumble over, again and again, hampering any enquiries. Whatever the stratum of society, rich or poor. Family loyalty so fierce and protective that getting at the whole truth and nothing but the truth was an impossibility.

'Do you consider the absence of a suicide note significant?'

She looked thoughtful, a fleeting expression as if something had occurred to her. A moment later it was gone.

'Surely it would have saved the family a great deal of anxiety and such enquiries as this would have been quite unnecessary if such a note had been written,' Faro prompted her.

She looked away, shook her head. 'I suppose so.'

It wasn't the answer he had hoped for. And, again feeling she had not been completely honest with him, he handed back the menu, which was impeccable, its ingredients innocent of venom. They had all eaten the meal, shared the same dishes. As for the wines served at the meal, they were innocuous, otherwise more than her brother-in-law would be now lying in Greyfriars Kirk. The fatal dose had been administered during that last hour Cedric and Theodore spent together.

And in this room.

All the time he was thinking: She could have done it easily. Slipped into this shadowy room unobserved. The serving table conveniently placed just inside the door, in order that an unobtrusive butler could attend to decanters and glasses without disturbing the two men sitting on either side of the fire. The armchairs Faro noticed had high backs, too, concealing the occupants from draughts and intrusions.

He reconstructed the scene. A noise, a door opening quietly, and neither man would have made the effort to sit up and look round, dismissing the newcomer as a soft-footed servant —

No, that would not do. What if Theodore had picked up the wrong glass?

If indeed Cedric had been poisoned by the claret, then his murderer had to have an accomplice. And if this lovely woman before him was the guilty one, then she had to have someone who would make sure that Cedric got the right glass. Someone she could trust.

A servant. Gimmond? Unlikely.

Then it could only be her husband. And Theodore

would lie and lie. As he Faro would have done had such a woman been his wife. He knew that, recognized it for his own weakness. That love – and loyalty – could be stronger than justice.

Switching from such uneasy thoughts, he asked: 'You must have known your brother-in-law very well. Granted that he thought he was incurably ill, did he ever show signs of mental disturbance? What I'm trying to say, did he ever hint that, let us say, if things got too bad, he might put an end to it all?'

'Never. No, never,' she replied quickly without the slightest hesitation, her eyes bright and shining, a slight smile playing about her lips intensifying that likeness to a Botticelli angel, as Faro had first seen her.

'When we – knew – what Cedric believed we were distraught. It was as if this death sentence had been passed on each one of us personally. There is nothing we would not do for each other, no sacrifice too great. We are that kind of family.'

In the silence that followed her words, for Faro could think of no rejoinder beyond a curt nod totally inadequate to the occasion, Barbara gazed up at the family portraits above the mantelpiece.

'That I think is the secret of how the Langweils have survived and prospered over so many centuries.'

When he declined the inevitable offer of tea, which seemed to be on hand at all hours in such houses, Faro recognized that it was also an indication that the interview was at an end.

About to take his leave, Barbara stood up saying she would accompany him.

Wrapping a shawl about her shoulders, she smiled. 'Just to the end of the drive. I would enjoy a little exercise. I get little chance these days. It is not the done thing for recently bereaved ladies to show their faces in public.'

Faro could think of nothing to say as they walked down the front steps. 'I understand you are from Orkney, Inspector. What brought you to Edinburgh?'

Faro told her, keeping his life story as brief as possible, certain that was not her reason for wishing to walk with him.

'That is very interesting,' she said. 'As for me, not even the wildest stretches of imagination could have prepared me for what my destiny held. My family were poor immigrants from Eastern Europe and we lived in direst poverty. I went to work as a waitress in a restaurant and it was there by the merest chance that Theodore Langweil, on a business visit to New York, and slumming it, you might say, came into my life. And stayed there.

'A fairy-tale story, is it not, Inspector? And yet so simple. Complete with happy ending. With Priorsfield – and all this – at the end of it. A happy devoted husband, and a loving family. What luck. Who could have imagined it?'

She turned and left him almost abruptly. He watched her go, walking lightly back towards the house.

Opening the gate of Priorsfield and shedding the enchanted spell of Barbara Langweil, he began to have his doubts.

There was something about so much loving, so much sweetness and light that he felt uneasily did not ring true to reality. It was the major obstacle in sniffing out murderers, rapists and petty criminals in a family circle. He thought again about loyalty. How even those who hated each other, screamed and railed and battered each other, or bore a lifetime's secret resentment, would lie and perjure rather than suffer the shame of seeing one of their kin sentenced to prison – and the noose.

If this was true of Edinburgh's poor, how much more so of the society where the good name was everything, the façade of a united family to be protected at all costs?

Squaring his shoulders with new determination he walked past Duddingston Loch, for in his eyes Barbara Langweil's proclamations of her family's apparent innocence took on a new meaning.

Surely her past was one of the Langweil family's best-

79

kept secrets? Why then had she confided in him this story of poor girl into rich wife? A simple story that any detective worth his salt knew perfectly well was all too often a motive and incentive for murder.

Chapter Nine

Unpleasantly wrapped in his own gloomy thoughts, Faro had reached the outskirts of Holyrood Park when he was hailed from a passing carriage.

It was Vince, accompanied by Grace and Rose. 'We are going out to the Golf Hotel for tea.'

'Do come with us, Papa. Please,' cried Rose.

'I ought to get back—' said Faro doubtfully.

'Oh, please, Papa. Vince, you make him come.' Rose persisted, reinforced by Vince's insistence.

And as they made room for him his stepson continued sternly: 'Time you stopped being so conscientious. Gave a little more time to the lighter things in life. I suppose you've been to Priorsfield.' And without waiting for an answer, 'That's enough activity for one day, surely?'

Faro glanced at Grace, awaiting her reaction. There was none. She merely adjusted her parasol, serenely regarding Salisbury Crags. 'These mild days are too good to miss.'

Her smile while a little lacking in her usual warmth was reasonably welcoming.

'We decided it was time we escaped from Edinburgh,' said Vince. 'It's my half-day off.' To which Grace glanced at Vince lovingly and tucked her arm into his, while Rose snuggled up close to her father and took his hand affectionately.

Sitting opposite the smiling couple in the carriage, Faro was both pleased and relieved by this return to the normal behaviour between them he had witnessed many times before Cedric's death. All was apparently well again between the two lovers.

At the hotel, Vince went to book in his guests with Rose skipping alongside. Grace, however, seemed glad of the opportunity to be alone with Faro.

'I'm so glad you came with us. I realize now how badly I have behaved and that it was quite silly to blame you – and my dear Vince – for doing what you thought was right.' She paused and looked towards the door where he had momentarily disappeared. 'I have always admired you for your integrity, you know that. And in similar circumstances I am sure I should have acted in exactly the same way myself.'

As Faro smiled down at her and took her hands she sighed. 'You see I do love Vince very much and I want to be his wife. Even if I do most earnestly hope – and believe – that you are mistaken and will find some perfectly innocent explanation of dear Papa's death.'

'We all hope that, my dear, I assure you.'

Grace looked at him gratefully and nodded. 'So Vince says. And you are so clever, he said we could rely on you to find out what really happened—'

As Vince reappeared with Rose, Grace took Faro's arm and, standing on tiptoe, kissed his cheek and whispered: 'I am still your devoted future daughter-in-law—'

'What's all this?' Vince said. 'Do I perceive a rival for my affections? Am I to call you out, sir?' he demanded mockingly. 'And you, madam, did I not observe you bestowing kisses on another man, and in public too?'

Grace prodded him in the ribs and seizing her he swung her off her feet, much to Rose's delight, while Faro observed this little pantomime with considerable relief. All was forgiven and he prepared to enjoy the afternoon tea, which was one of his weaknesses.

The hotel was famed for its Scotch pancakes, scones, and Dundee cake. Their table in the large window overlooked the course's rolling greens occupied by a few enthusiastic players, now straggling towards the hotel as the sun dipped low over the Pentlands.

And Faro was suddenly content, glad to be with the two happy young people who at that moment appeared to have not a care in the world. As for his dear Rose's presence, that was for him a wistful return to the domestic life which was increasingly one of his fleeting and ever retreating dreams.

Wednesday was half-day closing in Edinburgh and around them were other families with young children, enjoying the kind of life other men accepted as normal that he had so briefly known with a loving wife and bairns. He thought of Emily, seen, with luck, perhaps twice a year. Soon she too would be grown up like her sister, two young women with their own lives and dreams wherein he would have no part.

On to the peaceful scene beyond the window a dark shadow hovered, and as Faro lifted his second scone to his mouth a sparrowhawk swooped and with a scream of triumph ascended with its own ending to a hungry day's hunting.

Faro shuddered. There had been something ominous about that picture of sudden death which his three companions had not witnessed.

'Hello, Faro. You're a stranger.'

The deep voice at his elbow materialized as the manager of the hotel, an ex-colleague from the Edinburgh City Police. Peter Lamont's wife had been cook at a big house and when he retired, a hotel had been their particular ambition.

Vince and Grace after greeting him cordially returned to their own quiet chat.

Introduced to Rose, Lamont chuckled. 'Your daughter, eh, Faro? I remember you well, lass. I used to dandle you on my knee when you were a wee one.' And to Faro: 'Like to have a look round? We've made some improvements since we moved here a few weeks ago,' he said proudly.

'May I come too?' asked Rose.

'Aye, lass. Dr Laurie and Miss Langweil know the house well from the previous owners. They've been constant visitors.'

They followed him up the wide staircase into a handsome drawing room where visiting guests took their ease and then into the dining room overlooking the estuary of the River Forth.

'So that's where you are.' Mrs Lamont appeared clutching an armful of rolled papers. Seeing Faro again she flattered him by saying that he hadn't changed one scrap since she last saw him five, or was it six, years ago. 'How do you keep so slim and so young, Jeremy?' she said, eyeing her husband's corpulent figure and thinning hair.

Looking curiously at Rose, her eyes opened wide with astonishment. 'This young lady is never your daughter, Jeremy. Surely? My goodness.'

'I was just telling him that he ought to do a few rounds of golf to keep fit,' said Peter.

'He doesn't look as if he needs that. Besides, dear, it hasn't done much for you.'

'It's not the golf,' Peter grinned, 'it's all the ale and the appetite I have for your good food, dear.'

Mrs Lamont smiled at him. 'That's a very bonny lass your young Vince has got hold of.'

'We haven't seen so much of him since they got engaged.'

'I expect you will in the future. He's marrying into a golfing family, I understand.'

'And he could do a lot worse. We were right sorry to hear about her poor father.'

'Aye,' said Mrs Lamont. 'We'll miss them. Grand customers they were. Mr and Mrs Theodore and Mr and Mrs Cedric stayed with us in Perth too.'

Glancing at Faro and Rose, she chuckled. 'And talking of fathers too young-looking to have grown-up daughters, I really put my foot in it, thinking Mrs Cedric was far too young to have a lass the age of Miss Grace—'

'Then she realized that she must be her stepmother.' Peter's smiling interruption held a note of warning.

'Such a beautiful woman,' sighed Mrs Lamont.

No one could make that mistake. And Faro shook his head. 'I think you're confusing the two ladies. The young one is Mrs Theodore.'

'Oh – is she? Now that is interesting—'

Mrs Lamont looked quickly at her husband. 'That's even worse. Oh my goodness, how terribly embarrassing—'

'What was it you wanted, Betty?' Peter demanded rather sharply.

'Nothing, dear. I was just on my way to Room 37. I thought we might have enough of this paper' – she unrolled a length – 'to do that badly stained wall.'

'Let me see. Yes, I think that would do.'

'It was very expensive. Seems a shame to waste it.'

'May I see?' asked Faro. 'I recognize this one.'

'I expect you do, Jeremy. It was the rage in all the big houses about ten years ago. Fashions change and it's out of date now, of course, so we got a batch cheap when we moved into the hotel.'

Shaking hands with the manager and his wife, promises were exchanged to meet again soon. As they walked towards the staircase Faro asked Rose: 'Do we have that wallpaper in Sheridan Place?'

'No, Papa. I've never seen it before.'

'I have. And recently. Wish I could remember where.'

Rose chuckled. 'Dear Papa. Your much vaunted powers of observation and deduction never did reach the realm of ordinary things like clothes or decoration—'

'That, young lady, was a blow below the belt.'

She took his arm fondly. 'But you can't deny it. This is one case where you have to accept that you are guilty.'

From the landing they saw Vince helping Grace into her cloak. Setting off in the carriage once more they reached the outskirts of Edinburgh as a sunset glow touched the Pentlands with rose, echoing its majesty of crimson and gold on Arthur's Seat. A scene of tranquility and harmony outside, laughter in the carriage as Vince and Grace held hands and talked about their wedding plans.

'Papa, Grace would like Emily and me to be bridesmaids.'

Faro looked at Grace.

'As I have no sisters or girl cousins, it would make me very happy to have Vince's sisters. As long as you approve—'

Faro leaned over and took her hand. 'An excellent idea. And a very thoughtful one too.'

Here was an unexpected end to a routine working happy day, thought Faro. Vince and Grace had made up their differences, he had been reinstated and forgiven. He had renewed acquaintance with the past, an elderly couple with their lifetime's dream fulfilled, and before him sat a young couple whose happy future beckoned only a few months away.

He should have been happy. But he remembered other dark shadows: a sparrowhawk making its kill unobserved by all but himself, reminding him ominously that in the midst of life there is always sudden death. Death striking, unexpected and violent.

There was other residue from that afternoon's pleasant interlude which troubled him more. Lingering at the back of his mind, it refused to be banished. A case of mistaken identity perhaps but with such monstrous implications he could not bear to bring it into the light and scrutinize it closely.

For what he could not fail to recognize was its overwhelming significance in the murder of Cedric Langweil.

Sitting in his study that evening, he made a series of notes regarding his second line of enquiry: three people who had been present at the Priorsfield dinner party that fatal evening. None were witnesses to Cedric's demise but one had slept in the house that night.

As for the other two, their association with the Langweils might have some fact of vital importance to contribute.

He knew from years of past experience that it was often the seemingly innocent observation, the frailest of threads that he had followed, which had led his way out of the labyrinth to a confrontation with a murderer.

First on his list was the Langweil cousin, Reverend

Stephen Aynsley, who, Grace had told him, was now living with them until his plans were complete for going out to Africa.

Faro was relieved to find him at home in the town house, a visitor of sufficient importance to be allocated a handsome bedroom overlooking the Charlotte Square gardens.

When the maid announced Faro, Stephen Aynsley laid aside his Bible and received him graciously, not one whit put out when Faro said it was in connection with Cedric's death.

He nodded sadly. 'No need to apologize, Inspector. I am perfectly aware of police procedure in such matters. Of course you must talk to everyone who was in the house that night.' He smiled gently. 'For if my poor cousin was murdered, then we are all likely suspects, all capable of having criminal motives. None of us is safe.' Again he smiled. 'And it would not, I am sure, be the first time a clergyman has figured in your enquiries. All I can tell you is that I retired on the stroke of midnight. As I am a temperance man, my presence would have been an embarrassment long before Theo and Cedric began their serious drinking.'

Regarding Faro narrowly, he went on: 'Having said that, I have no witnesses for my departure except Theodore. I saw no one, rang for no hot milk. Nothing. Merely got into bed and was asleep, as is my wont, before my head touched the pillow. And you have only my word for that. After the servants retired, there was nothing to stop me from going quietly downstairs and slipping poison into Cedric's glass.'

Pausing, he gave Faro a triumphant look. 'As you will have observed the side table containing the decanters is very conveniently placed just inside the door. I could have done it easily. And so could – well, several other members of the household. Or a servant who had some mysterious reason, or some grudge, against his master. You look surprised, Inspector?'

Faro laughed. 'Only that I am wondering if you have chosen the right profession, sir.'

'Calling, Inspector. That's how we refer to it. We are called to the ministry.' He gave Faro a shrewd glance. 'There is one more vital question you have no doubt thought of? Surely the very first one that is in any policeman's mind. What have I to gain by my cousin's death?'

'I had thought of that, sir. That by nipping downstairs and putting poison in the wine you could have poisoned both Theodore and Cedric.'

'Ah yes. Now you are making sense. Although getting rid of poor Cedric would have availed me nothing. Polishing off both of them would have got me two steps closer to the Langweil fortune.'

He paused and then shrugged his shoulders. 'If I wanted it. Which I don't. You have to believe that. My destiny lies in Africa and although some money would undoubtedly have its uses in our mission work, I assure you it is not the kind that men murder for. Besides if we take this theory that I perhaps intended to murder both cousins, then it still does not make sense. I have not the least hope of inheritance unless the whole family is deceased. An impressive list, Inspector, including the expected new arrival in Adrian's household—'

At Faro's expression, he smiled. 'Adrian has just announced it. The family are delighted. And as I suspect this baby, if God wills it, to be the first of several, these are hardly the odds any sane man would take on, especially one with my modest expectations. One who believes in accordance with his mission, that poor as we are, if we have faith, then God will provide for our needs.'

Leaning across the table he said earnestly, 'I, for one, cannot believe the Langweils are capable of murder. The whole suggestion is too absurd even for outrage.' He laughed and shook his head. 'Of one thing I am absolutely sure, Inspector. Your investigations will prove only that they are innocent of Cedric's death.'

'What makes you so certain?'

Aynsley shrugged. 'You are much too clever a policeman not to have thought all that out for yourself. You have by now, I am sure, laid all the evidence in the case very neatly upon the table and examined it bit by bit and come to certain conclusions. Am I right?'

Faro regarded him thoughtfully. Surely a man of God should be more upset at the mortal sin of murder? Was his attitude not just a little too flippant for these serious allegations? Perhaps he would be wise to investigate the Reverend Stephen Aynsley a little more closely.

Aware of the other's smiling scrutiny, he shrugged: 'You are certainly very well informed for—'

'For a clergyman? Perhaps it seems a strange confession but I am particularly addicted to that form of literature. I am a great admirer of Poe, and Wilkie Collins and of course, even the late Mr Charles Dickens quite captivated me with his portrait of a detective, not unlike yourself, in *Bleak House*.'

'Inspector Bucket?'

'Ah, I see we share a similar taste in books, too.'

As they discussed the merits of Charles Dickens and Sir Walter Scott, Aynsley said: 'And there are the new scientific methods of detecting criminals. It must be extremely fortunate having a doctor at hand, especially one who I am given to understand served his apprenticeship with the police surgeon.'

As Faro prepared to leave, he asked: 'Have you any theories as to how your cousin died?'

Aynsley shrugged. 'Everything so far points to the possibility that Cedric took his own life. If so then there is one thing that does not make sense. Why did he leave no suicide note?'

'That has occurred to me.'

'I thought it would. Let me put to you, Inspector, that a man so devoted to his family would certainly have left some such evidence of his intention.' And shaking his head, 'Self-destruction is the most distressing exit from the world if one is a believer. In Cedric's case, the circumstances were understandable, but I find it difficult to believe or accept, knowing his deep family feeling, that he would not have left the simple explanation that would have saved any police investigation.'

When Faro walked down the steps of the Langweil house, he found himself the recipient of a handful of religious tracts and the distinct impression that Stephen Aynsley was labouring under the mistaken idea that Detective Inspector Faro had seen the light, bright as St Paul on the road to Damascus.

Not quite sure how he had found himself in such a situation or how the roles had been reversed, so that the detective-story reader Stephen Aynsley had asked the questions while he provided the answers, Faro had weakly left a handsome contribution to the Mission Fund with the certainty that if Aynsley could convert a man who hardly ever entered the doors of a church, then the heathens waiting in all their blissful ignorance in Africa were a walk-over.

As he staggered down the steps and pocketed his fistful of tracts, he shook his head sadly.

'I'm losing my grip, dammit,' he later told Vince, whose laughter at his stepfather's discomfiture was both long and hearty.

Next day, Faro walked down Albany Street to call on Piers Strong. He was received in an office where the architect was barely visible among the many and varied rolled-up plans which threatened every available inch of floor and desk space.

As the circumstances of Cedric's demise were still being kept secret, Faro had to choose his words carefully.

'I won't keep you, sir. There are some complications regarding Mr Langweil's sudden death.' At Piers' anxious expression he added hastily: 'Family business matters and so forth. It isn't all as straightforward as one might imagine.'

'Are you suggesting that it might be murder?'

'What makes you say that, sir?'

Piers shrugged. 'Why else would I be getting a visit from a detective inspector? Well, well. Pray continue.'

And the architect sat back in his chair regarding him eagerly. Obviously he wasn't used to such drama among his clients.

Before Faro could say another word, Piers interposed: 'Mind you, I have to say, I find the idea a bit hard to believe. They all seemed happy and so at ease. A devoted family even if tempers were raised over the proposed alterations – the new bathroom business – that is perfectly natural. I can vouch for it among many of my clients. Hardly enough to commit murder for, surely.'

When Faro made no comment Piers laughed. 'Mind you, I have men who would murder their wives rather than suffer all the inconvenience of a disrupted household. But that's only in small houses. Alterations in a place the size of Priorsfield would hardly be noticed. That's what I can't understand about Theodore's attitude. You'd think he'd want to please that young wife of his by letting her have everything up to date. In fact, you'd think he'd give her anything she asked for. And a bathroom wouldn't cost nearly as much as any of those lovely jewels she was wearing that night, I can tell you.'

Again he laughed. 'Now if it had been Theodore, there might have been a motive. Barbara is an absolute stunner, I'm sure there's men who'd commit murder to possess a wife as lovely as his missus.'

Faro looked at him thoughtfully. There seemed no reason for Cedric to have been murdered unless it was a desperate measure to prevent him changing his will.

Theodore's death made a lot more sense. And again he wondered, was he seriously on the wrong track. Had Cedric's death been a mistake. Had the poison been intended for his brother?

And if so, was the hand long and white, with exquisitely tapering fingers?

Chapter Ten

Faro's next call was on Mr Moulton, the Langweil lawyer. He felt that the old man received this visit with considerable caution and realized that getting him to part with any information concerning the family was not going to be easy.

The much-vaunted devotion and loyalty also extended to those they employed. A small, tight, impenetrable group.

Moulton's face remained expressionless as Faro repeated the reasons he had given Piers Strong for this enquiry.

'If it is about Mr Cedric's will, then I am afraid I cannot help you, Inspector,' he cut in sharply. 'We had only discussed the terms of the new will, it was in the process of being drawn up.' He spread his hands wide. 'The terms of the original will leaving his wife and daughter as benefactors now apply.'

'What were the terms of the new will?'

With a thin wintry smile, Moulton said: 'You have to realize, sir, that the lawyer is in much the same position as the priest in the confessional. And for your information I happen to be of the Roman Catholic persuasion.'

Realizing that Moulton probably knew more about the internal politics of the Langweil regime than anyone else, Faro decided to take him into his confidence.

'I quite understand, sir, your reasons are most commendable, but surely you would reconsider if you thought that Mr Cedric had been poisoned. And you would wish for the family's sake to help us find out who had murdered him.'

The old man shuddered. 'Murder,' he whispered. 'Such an idea is incredible. You cannot be serious, Inspector. Who on earth suggested such a thing to you?' he asked indignantly. And without waiting for Faro's reply, 'You must take my word for it, Inspector, I would be prepared to swear on one thing. That Mr Cedric died by his own hand.'

'For what reason?'

'His reasons appear patently obvious – to everyone but yourself, it appears. He believed that he was incurably ill, a dying man. Such conditions often make men's behaviour irascible, wondering when the fatal hour is to strike.'

'And what if I told you that he had never consulted any doctor, any reliable authority, to our certain knowledge, who confirmed his fears that he was incurably ill?'

Moulton looked worried. 'The important thing is that he believed it. Perhaps he lied to his family because he was afraid to face the truth. We all know, and I am sure your stepson can confirm this, that many people are afraid of doctors confirming their own suspicions and alas, die needlessly. We all have our Achilles' heel.'

'You say that Cedric was a caring man, sir. Then, in your own experience, do not most suicides leave a note of intent for their loved ones? Is it not curious that he omitted to do so?'

When the lawyer did not reply, Faro continued: 'You have known the family for many years.'

'I have indeed. I had the honour to serve Mr Theodore Langweil Senior.'

A new idea occurred to Faro. 'Perhaps then you know of the existence of something in the family's history that might have led Cedric to believe he was suffering from a brain tumour.'

A fleeting shadow touched the lawyer's face. 'I know of no such circumstances,' he said stiffly.

'What of the eldest son?'

'Justin, you mean? Gone long since,' Moulton replied sharply.

'You knew him then?'

93

'Of course I did. An unhappy young man. I hope he found his peace in America.'

His peace seemed a strange expression for the invalidish eldest son and heir of the Langweils.

Faro looked at Moulton quickly. His impression that the lawyer had not liked Justin Langweil was confirmed when the old man laughed harshly.

'Wilful and violent, perhaps such a nature fitted in better with the somewhat primitive conditions he sought in the wilds of California than with his respectable family background. You seem surprised, Inspector.'

'I am, a little, since such aspects of his character as you describe do not fit the description of the consumptive I have been given so far.'

'Who told you he was consumptive? He was – oh well,' Moulton shrugged, 'you had better get Mr Theodore to tell you all about Justin.'

'You make it sound very mysterious. And mysteries intrigue me, Mr Moulton.'

'I say no more, sir, than that he was not at all the sort of man the family would have been proud of. Quite different, thank God, to his brothers.' And eyeing Faro shrewdly, 'There's one in every pack, but young Justin was worse than the black sheep of the family. Much worse,' he added soberly.

'I can assure you of one thing, he left no broken hearts behind when he set sail for New York. As for not writing to them, that too was typical of the man. Thoughtless, uncaring, he had none of the sensitivity, the finer attributes, of the Langweils. From the day he walked out of Priorsfield, he literally shook its dust from his feet and has never communicated with any of them.'

A thought came into Faro's mind quite unbidden, a concept that would make quite a different story from the one he sought to untangle.

'Do you think there is any chance of him still being alive?'

Moulton frowned and then said quickly, 'Indeed, yes. Accidents and misinformation apart – as well as a hazardous mail service in that violent land – since he was just

94

two years older than Theo I should think there is every chance.' Giving Faro a curious look, he added: 'What are you thinking, Inspector?'

'Nothing important, sir.' But he left the lawyer's office thinking that the Langweil fortune might well be worth re-crossing the Atlantic for.

'And killing for,' he added later when he retold the day's interview for Vince's benefit.

'Justin Langweil. The black sheep of the family,' Vince whistled. 'Of course I've heard about him, Stepfather. In suitably hushed tones.'

'And what have you heard?'

'Well, you know what it's like. The family aren't exactly proud of him, they prefer to draw a veil over his early life, bit of a hell-raiser, I gather. I didn't know of his existence for a long time, they like to give the impression publicly that there were only three sons and that the eldest had died in infancy. Then Grace told me that she gathered that he had gone to America long ago. Naturally she was very curious, got this romantic idea of a rakehell uncle who had thrown away his birthright for a life of adventure.'

Pausing, he grinned. 'Grace is very addicted to novel-ettes with heroes who rush off, endure terrible hardships, and return in time to save the family fortune – and marry a rich second cousin.'

He stopped, frowning at his stepfather's look of pre-occupation. 'Do I understand rightly that you are toying with some notion that Justin might be very much alive and lurking around Priorsfield waiting for the right moment to make a dramatic entrance? The prodigal son returned. But in this case, judging from what Moulton told you, I think the fatted calf could breathe easy. There wouldn't be much rejoicing.'

He was silent for a moment then said: 'There's only one flaw in this argument, Stepfather. If your assumption is right then Justin Langweil can walk in any day of the week and reclaim his inheritance. All he needs is to prove his identity. There is absolutely no reason for him to kill anyone or to poison Cedric – Theodore would make more sense if that was his intention – to repossess what any court will say is rightfully his. So why put his neck in danger?'

'There is one good valid reason for him returning incognito which we must not overlook.'

Vince thought for a moment. 'You mean that he might have a criminal record in America? Sounds just that sort of fellow from Moulton's description too. Could that have been what he meant by "misinformation"?'

Faro nodded and both men were silent considering this new aspect of the case.

At last Vince said: 'On the other hand, Moulton could be right about Cedric having done away with himself. Adrian is still very upset about the whole business, as you can well imagine. Cedric was his older brother, closer to him than Theodore. He's going to miss him. He shares Moulton's opinion, mine too, for what it's worth, despite the absence of any suicide note.

'Adrian was telling me that Cedric was morbidly interested in poisons, not just in a general way, he used to read books about poisoners and their methods.'

But it was Sergeant Danny McQuinn who unearthed a completely new motive in his conscientious interviewing of Maud Langweil's household. Getting his feet under the table, he called it, he was now on first-name terms with the housekeeper, Mrs Molly Bates.

'There I was, sir, sitting cosy like by the fire, enjoying a rare cup of tea when the kitchen door opened and an ancient crone sidled in.

'Molly introduced us. This was her cousin Bess and Bess's proud boast was that she had been wet-nurse to Justin and Theodore. So between the two of them there was quite a bit of family gossip. Not particularly interesting to begin with: "D'ye mind the second cousin of old so-and-so – well, he's deid." That sort of thing. But I'm a good listener, Inspector. I believe in keeping my ears open, and I was rewarded. It wasn't until the old lass said how sorry she's been about poor Mr Cedric. And shaking her head, how history repeated itself.

'I sat up at that. The whisper had got around the servants that the master had done himself in.

' "Just like poor Mr Justin's young wife."

' "Say that again," says I. And she didn't take much persuasion to tell the whole story. I'll keep it nice and short for you, Inspector.

'Apparently when Mr Justin was about eighteen, he brought a lassie home, claimed they were wed, even produced the lines. But it was plain as plain, according to old Bess and the rest of the family, that she had trapped him. Wasn't in their class at all. Well, she didn't last long.

'The old biddy used to go in and do a bit of ironing for them and the lassie often came into the kitchen in floods of tears. Mr Justin used to use his fists on her. "He always was a bully, even as a wee laddie," says old Bess.

'Well, one day, she put an end to it all. Topped herself. The family hushed it up, of course, and Justin left for America. Heart-broken and full of remorse, they said.'

'Wait a minute, McQuinn. How could they hush it up? Surely there was an enquiry. When was this, anyway?'

'Hold on, sir. I'm coming to that. According to old Bess, everyone believed she had died of a fever.'

So they got a doctor more willing than Vince to sign a false death certificate, thought Faro grimly.

'You won't find anything,' McQuinn continued quickly. 'I've looked.'

'Strange I never heard about it. Never even heard it mentioned.'

'It was before your time. Year before you joined the force. Looked up the records and there's nothing. No enquiry, nothing. Money can buy such things, as you know, sir, for those in high places. But I thought you'd be interested.'

'I am indeed. Especially since I doubt whether even Vince knows that Justin had a wife who did away with herself. Thanks, McQuinn, this does change the picture.'

*

When Faro returned home that evening it was with almost a feeling of guilt that he had been in the house for some time going over his notes without asking where Rose was.

Matters were not improved when Mrs Brook brought in his supper.

'Miss Rose, sir? Why, she has gone to stay at Charlotte Square with Miss Grace overnight.'

Faro bit back his anger and disappointment. When Vince arrived he said: 'Of course I'm not objecting, but surely I should have been consulted first.'

'Not very easy, Stepfather, I took it on myself to give permission. Thought you wouldn't mind, seeing that you are so seldom at home.'

It was true. He had hardly seen Rose since the weekend they had spent together, a fact which did nothing to lessen his feelings of guilt. He had longed for his daughter's visit but realized he had seriously neglected her ever since.

'You seem to forget I am involved in a murder case.' The words were out before he realized how tactless and hurtful they were, especially as that same case stemmed from within the house where his daughter was staying.

Was that what troubled him most of all?

Vince put a hand on his shoulder. 'Any progress?'

Faro threw down his notes and sighed. 'Every new factor just adds new complication. Did you know that Justin had a wife?'

'A wife? Heavens, no.'

'I thought Grace might have told you.'

'I'm sure she would have done so, if she'd known. She's always given the impression that he was just a lad when he rushed off.'

'Even a lad of eighteen can take a wife.'

'This is news. Tell me about her.'

When Faro finished the story McQuinn had told him, Vince whistled. 'I'm sure Grace doesn't know any of this. Not exactly a piece of family history the Langweils would be proud of.'

'I think you might discover that a lot of things have been kept from Grace, for her own good – they would say.'

In the silence that followed Vince stared at him. 'Do you think Justin might still be alive then?'

'Not only alive but in Edinburgh. And a possible suspect.'

'You mean, you think he might have had something to do with Cedric's death. But why and more important, how? I mean, it just doesn't make sense, if he is alive then he is the legitimate heir so why all the secrecy—'

'Necessary if, as we discussed earlier, he has a criminal record.' And before Vince could interrupt, he went on: 'As a matter of fact I was thinking along quite different lines. In the light of McQuinn's discovery, we have a new motive for his return – incognito.'

'I see what you mean. Revenge—'

'Aye, revenge. Something we'd never even thought of. An execution sentence on the Langweils for the death of his young wife who made her so unhappy she took her own life.'

'Wait a moment. Adrian couldn't be guilty, he was just a boy then. The only ones who could be blamed were Theodore – and Cedric. God save us.'

Pausing he looked across at Faro. 'I've heard of cases like this. If Justin was mad, or bad, enough—Do you know, Stepfather, nothing in this case has made sense so far, but now, maybe there is something in what you're suggesting.'

Faro lit a pipe and watched the smoke ascending. Poor Vince, he was pathetically eager to find a new scapegoat for Cedric's death. 'He had to gain access to the house. And seeing that Theodore and Cedric might recognize him, even after twenty years, what would be his easiest way of entering the Langweil house?'

'As a servant?'

'Precisely. People like the Langweils never look twice at servants.'

'And once he was inside, the rest was easy – well, moderately easy. There's only one thing I don't understand, Stepfather. Poison was put into one glass only, when he could have just as easily used the opportunity to get rid of both of them.'

'Perhaps that was part of a diabolical plot, that he wanted to poison one brother and have the other blamed.'

Vince looked at him, shook his head. 'I just can't take any of this as a serious proposition. I'm sorry, Stepfather, it's too far-fetched for me.'

Faro knocked the ashes from his pipe. 'You're probably right, lad. What is it we say? Discard all the impossibles and what remains must be the truth.' He stood up wearily. 'All I know is that somehow we've got off the right track. We have to begin again, sift through the evidence, starting with the servants' hall at Priorsfield.'

Early next morning, Faro called on Theodore Langweil, and asked him for a list of their domestic servants, indoors and out.

'Is this to do with my brother's death?'

'Perhaps, sir.'

'Very well. Anything to get this accursed enquiry settled. However,' he added drawing a ledger from his desk drawer, 'I can assure you that you won't find your murderer, if such a creature exists, in this household.'

Opening the pages he said: 'Where would you like to begin?'

'My sergeant, with your permission, will copy down the names and the lengths of time they have been in your service.'

'Is that all?' said Theodore heavily. 'And your sergeant—'

'McQuinn, sir. He will be arriving later today to talk to them. All I need from you are the long-term servants who need not be interviewed. Those who have been with you more than twenty years. Before your eldest brother went to America.'

'Oh, indeed.' Theodore was suddenly very still. Watchful, thought Faro. Suspicious. And he was sure that he had also turned a shade paler. 'What is all this about?' he rapped out sharply.

'Certain facts have come to our notice—'

'Facts? What kind of facts?' Theodore demanded.

'Concerning your brother Justin. Look, sir, we know

100

that he had a young wife, who did away with herself.'

Theodore winced. 'That is not true. Her death was accidental.' But he looked frightened.

'How did she die?'

'I am not prepared to discuss that with you, Inspector. It has no connection with your enquiry. Let us just say she was a very disturbed and unhappy young woman. And leave it at that.'

'I must disagree with you sir. It could have quite a lot to do with Cedric's death. If Justin is still alive.'

For the first time Theodore looked frightened. 'I assure you Justin is dead. Long since.'

Theodore had recovered his composure. His scornful laugh and his tone were emphatic. 'Before you go to any more ridiculous lengths of alarming my staff and the rest of my family, let me assure you, Justin is dead.'

'Have you proof of that, sir?'

'Only that the gold camp where he was prospecting was overrun by renegade Indians. The white men were tortured to death. And Justin was one of them.'

'How do you know all this? The story I heard was that your brother had disappeared and never communicated with you.'

Theodore smiled sadly. 'Nor did he. That was true. Cedric and I agreed not to distress the family by revealing the true facts regarding Justin's ending.' Unlocking a drawer in his desk, he handed Faro a folded paper, yellowed and dog-eared.

It was headed: 'A true copy of a letter from Messrs Mace and Mace, Bush Street, San Francisco', and dated February 1856:

Dear Sir—

Our exhaustive investigations on your behalf into the disappearance of your brother Justin Langweil have now revealed that he was murdered by Indians . . .

Faro skimmed the remaining paragraph, which was in essence what Theodore had told him.

He handed it back and shook his head. 'I'm sorry, sir.'

'No need for condolences, Inspector. Justin was no adornment to this family, but the search had to be made. In order that certain business matters be cleared.'

He paused, then added, 'If you wish for additional proof, then Moulton our lawyer has the original letter. In a sealed envelope marked private and confidential.'

'Moulton does not know the contents of this letter?'

Theodore shrugged. 'No, why should he? There are matters concerning the family which are no business of his.'

So Theodore didn't even trust the old family lawyer. What was it Moulton had called it: 'misinformation'? Did he suspect the truth. Or was Theodore lying? Again.

There was one way of finding out.

Chapter Eleven

Eager to hear McQuinn's report on the Priorsfield servants, Faro returned to his office later that day. Expecting
to find him alone he was surprised to hear feminine laughter as he opened the door. Throwing it open, the last
person he expected to see there was leaning across his
desk.

It was Rose. Rose, happy and animated, her face
flushed with pleasure. Danny McQuinn wore an
expression of wry amusement and it was some moments
before the young sergeant became aware of Faro glower-
ing in the background.

Springing to his feet, he saluted smartly. 'Morning, sir!'

Rose turned, smiled delightedly. 'Papa! I've been waiting for you.'

'What are you doing here?' Faro asked.

'I came to see you, of course.' Anyone but Rose would
have detected a certain steely quality had crept into her
father's voice. 'Sergeant McQuinn has been very
hospitable.'

'Has he indeed?' And ignoring the unhappy-looking
sergeant, Faro said: 'Well, I am here. What is it you
want? I thought you were staying with Miss Langweil.'

'Just for one night, Papa. I decided as the carriage was
passing close by your office that I would look in and see
you. Just for a few moments. I'm usually in bed when
you get home in the evenings.'

Although there was no reproach in Rose's statement,
Faro was again guiltily aware that he had sorely neglected
his daughter on this visit.

Looking round his office, each shelf stacked high with documents, she commented: 'It is years since the last time I was in here. It hasn't changed much, has it? They don't spend much on paint and paper, do they? And you still have the same books on the shelves, in exactly the same places. Do you ever open them?'

'Rose dear,' he interrupted, conscious of McQuinn's knowing smile, 'what was it you wanted? Are you short of cash?'

'No. Do I have to have a reason to look in and say hello to my Papa?'

Faro forced a smile. 'I appreciate your visit, Rose, but I do have rather a busy morning, a lot of matters—'

'To attend to,' she completed with a sigh. 'But then you always have, Papa.'

Faro looked at McQuinn who, for once it seemed, proved not insensitive to a delicate situation. Gathering his papers together, he bowed to Rose. 'Morning, Miss,' and went towards the door.

'On your way out, McQuinn, be so good as to summon a carriage to take Miss Faro home.'

As the door closed on him, Rose said: 'I'm sorry if you are cross about me going to stay with Grace. Since I spend most of the day with her anyway. And it also means that I see Vince in the evenings.' She shook her head sadly. 'It isn't working out the way I thought it would. I mean, you are busy, Vince is busy, and I do get very bored staying indoors.'

'I thought you loved Sheridan Place. The number of times you've begged to come and stay with me,' he emphasized the last words.

'So I have, Papa. But in the past I've always had Emily. And I do miss having a companion of my own age. I didn't realize that I'd be staying with Mrs Brook. Not that I object to her, for she is a dear person, but we haven't a great deal in common and she has lots to do with the house to run. I can hardly expect her to chaperone me every time the sun shines and I want to walk in the park or look at some shops!'

As she spoke, Faro for the first time saw himself mirrored in her eyes as a selfish, thoughtless parent. He wanted his daughter when he was available to be with her, not caring that she might have to sit in an empty house waiting for him to come home. With a pang of remorse, he realized that her poor mother, his dear faithful Lizzie, had also spent her life waiting for a husband who was always late for meals and never around when she needed him.

He should have been glad that Rose had made friends, and with Grace Langweil. But he wasn't. The idea of having his daughter stay in a house whose occupants were under the shadow of murder continued to make him uneasy.

A knock on the door and McQuinn said: 'Carriage is here for Miss Rose, sir.'

Taking her by the arm, Faro led her along the corridor and into the street, aware that she looked around smiling, hoping to see McQuinn, and clearly disappointed when he tactfully remained invisible.

Putting her into the waiting carriage, Faro kissed her and said, 'We'll talk about this later, my dear.'

'Promise?'

'Promise.'

McQuinn had returned to the office and was waiting for him.

'Storm in a tea cup, sir?' he grinned.

Faro nodded and said: 'Let's get down to business. We've wasted enough time.'

And he launched into an account of the latest developments of the Langweil case.

McQuinn handed him the list of servants. 'I think that rather settles any ideas we might have that the missing brother is lurking about. There isn't anyone who could remotely be Justin Langweil in disguise. All the middle-aged men are gardeners and malthouse workers. They have been there since they were lads. I'll say it for the Langweils, their staff think well of them. No grumbles from below stairs either. So where do we go next, sir?'

105

Faro considered the list. 'I want you to find out from everyone at Priorsfield, never mind if they have told you already – ask them to repeat it, every detail they can remember from the moment the visitors left the house the night of Cedric's death until they retired to bed.'

McQuinn whistled. 'That's a tall order, sir. It wasn't yesterday, exactly.'

'I know. But do it.'

McQuinn went to the door and turned. 'I don't get the drift, sir. Do you think Justin Langweil—'

'Never mind what I think, McQuinn. Let's say I'm just not satisfied with the evidence so far. There's something missing. Something that has been overlooked. Someone's not telling the absolute truth and I suspect either concealing by accident or design some vital clue. And we're damned well going to find it, even if it means raising a hornets' nest in the ranks of a loyal and devoted family.' He stood up, gathered his notes together. 'Meanwhile, I'm going to see their lawyer again.'

And see him again Faro did. But not quite as he had expected to. A call at the office revealed that Mr Moulton was seeing a client in East Lothian and was not expected back until later that day.

The weather took a turn for the worse. The mild spring-like days disappeared in rain sheets and a furious gale rattled the windows in Sheridan Place, and sent gusts of smoke billowing down the chimneys.

Even on calm nights, Faro was finding difficulty in sleeping soundly and the sudden unexpected storm did nothing for his composure or his ability to wrestle with the baffling elements of the Langweil murder.

Early the following morning, an unforgivably cheerful and healthy-looking McQuinn arrived at Sheridan Place while Faro was breakfasting with Vince and Rose.

'Forgive the interruption, sir.'

Rose was clearly delighted. 'How nice to see you, Sergeant. Have you had breakfast?'

'I have, miss. But thank you kindly—'

'You will surely have some tea with us?'

Before Faro could protest, McQuinn smiled and shook his head. 'Sorry, miss, another time perhaps.' And to Faro: 'I'm on my way to Duddingston, sir. Thought you'd want to come with me. And you, Dr Laurie. You may be needed.'

McQuinn's expression indicated serious police business, not to be discussed in front of young ladies.

His manner was urgent enough for Faro and Vince to jump up from the table and follow him into the hall.

'What has happened?' Faro demanded.

'That lawyer, Moulton, has been found floating in the loch.'

As the police carriage hurtled through Holyrood Park, McQuinn told them that a farmer on his way to market had spotted a wrecked carriage at the bottom of the steep incline they were approaching.

'It had its wheels in the air and the horse was still in its traces but looked as if it was dead. He was curious so he went down for a better look. And there beside it floating in the waters was a man's body.'

A small crowd had already gathered at the water's edge. The three men slithered down to join them through the wet grass, for there had been heavy rain during the night. Faro recognized with a sickened sense of disaster the two-wheeler that he had last seen outside Moulton's office.

Vince was bending over the body. After a brief examination he said: 'I should estimate he's been dead for less than twelve hours.'

'That would make it about midnight.' And staring at the front of Priorsfield across the other side of the loch, Faro frowned. 'I wonder what he was doing on the road at that time of night.'

'I can tell you that, sir.'

The speaker was a rough-looking fellow, a stableman by his attire.

'I work at Priorsfield. Mr Moulton was visiting the

master and he came round for his carriage about midnight.' Leaning forward confidentially, he shook his head. 'Had quite a bit to drink, by the look of him, though one shouldn't talk ill of the dead and an old 'un like that. Fair staggering he was and in a bit of a paddy. Fair whipped up his horse, too, he did as they trotted off down the drive. Far too old—'

But Faro was no longer listening. 'Tell my sergeant here, will you? What's your name? Jock. Very well, Jock, and while you're here, would you take a look at the wreckage?'

'Oh, I can tell you what caused the accident. The wheel came off. First thing I did when I came down—'

'And how did the wheel come off?'

The man shook his head. 'No idea, sir. The pin was broken. Might have been wear, but I didn't notice any wobble on it as the gentleman left – of course, it could have—'

'Hold a minute, if you please. Look,' Faro interrupted, moving rapidly in McQuinn's direction, 'take this fellow's statement. I don't suppose anyone saw the accident, no one would be on the road in a storm like that.'

'Unlikely, sir. Folks unfortunate enough to be out walking would be keeping their heads well down—'

McQuinn paused as Faro stared at the white-faced house across the loch. 'Do I take it you don't think it was an accident, sir?'

'See what you think when you've had the stableman's story, McQuinn. I'm off to see Mr Langweil.'

By the time the police carriage had reached the house by circumnavigating two sides of the loch any element of surprise was lost.

Theodore had been walking his dogs and the two Labradors bounded up the front steps to greet Faro. Their master looked genuinely concerned at Faro's arrival.

'Come in, Inspector. I suppose it's about poor old Moulton. One of the servants has just told me. What a tragedy.'

And ushering him into the library, he closed the door, poured himself a drink.

'May I offer you some refreshment, Inspector?'

'Too early in the day for me, sir,' said Faro with a faintly disapproving look at the decanter and wondering if Theodore Langweil normally began imbibing whisky at ten in the morning. Or was it comfort for a very frightened man?

'I understand that Mr Moulton visited you late last night.'

'Yes, he did. Who told you that?' demanded Langweil idly.

'Your stableman. He saw Mr Moulton leave.'

Theodore sighed. 'Then he probably told you that the old man was somewhat the worse of drink.' Without waiting for Faro's comment, he continued: 'I warned him. But he was a headstrong old devil. Never listened to a word of warning from anyone that driving a two-wheeler at a reckless speed at his age – and in a drunken condition—'

'May we go back to the beginning of the evening, sir? May I enquire, what was the reason for his visit?'

Theodore's lip curled. 'Is this an official enquiry, Inspector? I mean, does anyone who visits this house have to have a reason, other than a social occasion?'

When Faro did not answer, Theodore sighed wearily. 'All right. Old – I mean, Mr Moulton, came because I asked him to do so. There were various business matters to discuss, that have been delayed since my brother's death. He no longer conducts his business at any great speed, you understand.'

'At what time did he arrive?'

Theodore thought. 'About seven. He left again around midnight.'

'You must have had a great deal to discuss,' Faro said heavily.

Langweil's face was expressionless. 'We did.'

'And might I presume that the urgency of his visit was somehow connected with the original of the letter from San Francisco which you showed me earlier in the day—'

'Damn your eyes, Faro,' Langweil exploded. 'Of course

109

it wasn't. I – I did—' and then again he sighed, mollified. 'I did mention it to him in passing, of course, just ensuring its safety, and he told me that it was locked in his office safe with the rest of the family documents.'

'So after you had finished discussing urgent matters, you turned to more convivial things.'

'Naturally. Old Mouldy had a rich treasure of wicked tales from behind the scenes in so-called respectable Edinburgh. I always enjoy listening to his stories. Besides, the weather was foul. A sudden storm of rain and hail. We hoped it would settle and when it did not, I invited him to stay the night. But he refused. He insisted on getting home to his own bed.'

Langweil thumped his fists together angrily, as if the full force of the tragedy had suddenly struck a chord of emotion. 'Fool of a man, he would still have been alive if he'd taken my advice – for once.'

'When he left, did you see him off?'

'On a night like that?' Theodore looked amused. 'Why, that is what servants are for, Inspector.'

'Your stableman Jock said Mr Moulton was in a rage. Thought he was very upset about something.'

'Did he indeed? If the stupid fellow had used his head, he would have realized that any old gentleman, known at the best of times for his crusty temper, would have been upset and in a rage at the prospect of driving an open carriage back to Edinburgh in a hailstorm. You must have heard it in Newington?'

And Theodore stood up indicating that the interview was at an end. As they walked across the hall, he asked: 'Any idea what caused the accident?'

'A broken wheel pin, I gather.'

Theodore nodded. 'I thought it couldn't be just Moulton's reckless driving.'

At the front door, Faro paused. 'Tell me, Mr Langweil, did you have any reason for leaving the house last night?'

'Last night? Of course not, I was entertaining Mr Moulton.'

'Precisely that, sir. I mean during his visit.'

110

Langweil looked at him as if he had taken leave of his senses. 'I don't understand what you're getting at, Inspector. There was a storm raging outside. I had a guest.'

And bidding him good day Faro rapidly walked towards the police carriage with the satisfaction of seeing Langweil's expression change to one of open-mouthed astonishment as if the significance of the question had just dawned.

Theodore was either an exceedingly accomplished actor or else he was innocent. And if he was innocent there existed a strong possibility that someone else had hastened the old lawyer to his untimely end.

A possibility Faro viewed without any relish, that he might now have a second murder case to solve.

The carriage dropped him outside the consulting rooms Vince shared with Adrian Langweil, where the latter had just heard the news and was very upset. It seemed that of all the brothers he was fondest of the old lawyer, who had always made a great fuss of him.

'He was like a father to me,' he said gloomily, 'I shall miss him.'

Having found Adrian alone and without any appointments for the next half-hour Faro decided to take full advantage of the situation. The time was long past when he felt obligated to respect Theodore's desire to protect the Langweil family by withholding vital information concerning the missing brother Justin.

Perhaps there was indeed something Adrian was aware of, but had not put into words, which might give Faro the lead he so desperately needed. But at the end of his disclosure about the letter from the San Francisco lawyers, Adrian sighed. 'Poor old Justin. And yet, I'm not really surprised, you know. Good of Theo to try to spare us, but I always had the strangest feeling that Justin had gone for ever, that he would never come back from America.'

'How curious. Had you any reasons for this?'

111

'None at all. But even when I was quite a little lad I had the feeling that Justin was dead. And that something quite dreadful had happened to – something terrible—'

He paused, biting his lips. 'It was like trying to remember a dream – a nightmare.'

'Could it have been a whispered conversation you over-heard about Justin, between your brothers?'

Adrian brightened. 'You might well be right about that. I was a sore trial to them in that I was a bad sleeper, still am, and I used to prowl about Priorsfield in the middle of the night – with a lighted candle – searching for Prince Charlie's lost gold.'

He smiled at Faro. 'You know what children are like, Mr Faro. I got this bee in my bonnet, I was addicted to adventure stories and I got this idea that someday I would find the secret of that lost French gold.'

'I thought the legend was that the French count missed the Prince. That they never met.'

Adrian shrugged. 'I know that. But it didn't satisfy me. I remembered that the rightful heir to the Scottish throne had visited this house constantly when his troops were camped on Arthur's Seat before the Battle of Preston-pans. It was marvellous ground for a young lad's romanc-ing. And then there was the murdered man – the skeleton they dug up in the grounds—'

Faro smiled. This was a new and surprising aspect of the hard-headed doctor.

'There was – probably still is – a trunk full of dressing-up costumes, old clothes dating way back into the last century,' Adrian continued dreamily. 'In my satin waist-coat and knee breeches I tried to will myself into seeing what Priorsfield was like in those days. It wasn't until my niece Grace was a little girl that I discovered I had a soul mate, someone who shared my feelings that the house was, well, haunted.'

Faro looked at him. 'Yes, Vince said something of the sort.'

'She had better luck than I ever did, although it almost scared her to death. She saw – or claimed she saw, no one believed her but me – the ghost of a man, in the costume of the last century. She saw him more than once—'

Now Faro remembered. 'That was the reason she would never sleep there alone.'

'Oh, how I envied her. I would have given anything to see her ghost. When I think how I used to sit on the stairs and try to escape back into the past.'

A tap on the door interrupted him, announcing the arrival of his next patient.

'How did we get on to all this, Mr Faro? We've come a long way from whatever it was you wanted to know. But I've enjoyed chatting to you.'

Faro went away very thoughtfully. Adrian's story had brought him no nearer to finding the truth about Justin Langweil. This might be an opportune time to visit the old lawyer's office. He had a sudden urgent desire to see the original of that San Francisco letter.

He found Mr Wailes, the lawyer's assistant, in sole occupation of the office. Referred to by Mr Moulton as his 'young clerk', Faro was surprised to see that he was nearer fifty than the twenty years such a description would have merited.

When Faro announced himself as calling in connection with the accident, Mr Wailes regarded him gravely.

He looked very upset, near to tears, hovering over Moulton's possessions returned by the police and spread on the table before him.

'I cannot believe that he has gone, Inspector. He was such a brave, gallant old man—'

Faro listened sympathetically to a eulogy far removed from the irascible crusty old gentleman who left his mark upon the inhabitants of Priorsfield over the years.

Finally he interrupted. 'I wonder if you could help us. I have just been to Priorsfield and Mr Theodore wishes urgently to have confirmation of a document from the family papers.'

It was taking a long shot indeed, Faro realized as both

he and Wailes stared at the bunch of keys which had never left Moulton's person until his death.

'Mr Moulton never let them out of his possession for an instant,' said Wailes, doubtfully touching them in the awed manner of a sacred relic. 'In all my years here, I have never opened that safe, nor do I know exactly what it contains.'

He paused, frowning. 'But I suppose now that I am in charge of the office until the terms of Mr Moulton's will have been read and discharged—' Pausing, he sighed.

'There may well be other clients with urgent business,' said Faro, realizing that he was taking a mean advantage of the man's distress.

'That is true, sir. Very true. Might as well make a start.' For a moment he hesitated, then picking up the keys he looked at them as if they might burn a hole in his hand:

'Well, sir, at least I have the law present in case anyone should suggest what I did was improper.'

The contents of the shelves were very neatly labelled, as Faro might have suspected: the old lawyer had been a very methodical man. The files were all arranged in alphabetical order from which Wailes withdrew that marked 'Langweil'.

'What was it you wished to see, Inspector?'

Faro told him he was looking for a letter from lawyers in San Francisco, marked private and confidential.

'There's only one sealed document here. "To be opened by Adrian Langweil in the event of the death of Theodore and Cedric Langweil." Looks like a will, sir.'

'That can't be it.'

He stared over Wailes' shoulder as the clerk skimmed through the old documents, many of which must have dated back to the original deeds of Priorsfield. But they, though of antiquarian interest, were none of his business.

'You are quite sure of the date?'

Faro did not need to consult his notes to know that the date was right and that if Moulton had exceeded his authority by removing it from its envelope then he would also have filed it in the proper sequence.

114

Three times Wailes went through the documents. Finally he shook his head. 'I'm sorry, Inspector. There is no such letter in the file. And you have my assurance that if Mr Moulton had it in his possession, it would have been here – right here, sir.'

Pausing he looked at Faro. 'I can only suggest, sir, that Mr Langweil has made a mistake and that you take up the matter with him again. Twenty years is a long time. Perhaps he reclaimed the document for some purpose and forgot to return it to Mr Moulton. That does happen with clients sometimes.'

Thanking him for his help, Faro walked down the front steps sure of one thing: that the original had never existed except in the fabric of Theodore Langweil's imagination.

At the Central Office, McQuinn looked in to see him later that day.

Handing him the statements from the farmer who had found the lawyer's body and the stableman Jock, he said: 'I decided to have another talk to the servants at Priorsfield.

'This will interest you, sir. Mrs Gimmond was grumbling about the hailstorm and the awful weather, especially as she had to give one of the maids a good ticking off. The lass had been in tears, swearing she had polished the front hall floor and that it had been left beautiful.

' "Well," said Mrs G, 'it wasn't beautiful when I came downstairs this morning. There were muddy footprints all the way to the library and up the stairs. The master would have had a fit if he'd seen them when he came down to breakfast. A stickler for polished floors he is. Worse than the mistress." '

McQuinn sat back in his chair and regarded Faro triumphantly. 'So what do you think of that, sir?'

'I'd give a lot to know in which direction the muddy footsteps were going.'

McQuinn scratched his chin. 'I think I can give you an answer to that, too. Remember the storm didn't start until ten o'clock. By then Mr Moulton was with Mr

Langweil. He was the only guest, the only one to leave the house.'

'Wait a moment, McQuinn.' And Faro remembered having asked Langweil if he had seen his guest off.

'Well, sir, he lied. He or someone else must have been out of the house some time that evening after they ate. And it wouldn't be one of the servants because the footsteps were leading to the library and upstairs. A servant would have gone through the baize door downstairs.'

'You're right. And if Langweil left the house in the storm, he had a purpose.'

McQuinn smiled. 'Like tampering with the wheel of the lawyer's carriage and then filling him with drink so that he'd be right fuddled on that twisting road by the loch.'

When Faro related the day's events to Vince, he saw by his stepson's expression that he still hoped for a miracle and that Grace's family would somehow be declared innocent of what now looked like two murders.

'I'm particularly interested in Justin Langweil. Especially after what Adrian told you.'

'Oh, I haven't given up hope that we'll unearth him yet.'

'He is certainly the most likely candidate.'

Vince sounded almost hopeful. After all the lad had a bad reputation, better the black sheep than one of the respectable Langweils.

Faro slept little that night. Eventually he got up and brought up to date his notes on the case. Throwing down his pen, he was no further out of the labyrinth.

All the evidence pointed to Theodore being guilty of murdering Cedric and then the old lawyer because he knew too much.

The other idea, ever growing in magnitude, was that the missing eldest brother was very much alive and well in Priorsfield.

There was one other possibility, so obvious that it never even occurred to him to give it a serious thought.

116

Chapter Twelve

Returning home preoccupied with the day's events but determined to set them to one side for Rose's benefit, he was disagreeably surprised to find that he had a visitor.

McQuinn was sitting in the dining room and Rose was talking to him in her usual animated fashion.

Soft-footed as always, they did not immediately observe his arrival on the scene. But seeing them together smiling and happy, he realized with a pang that whereas twelve years might seem a vast difference between a girl of fifteen and a man of twenty-seven, as a couple grew older so did the odds diminish.

And standing there unobserved he remembered that Lizzie had been Rose's age when, a servant in the 'big house', she had been seduced by one of the aristocratic house guests.

Vince had been the result of that tragic ill-fated episode.

A shiver of apprehension went through Faro. That situation must not be allowed to repeat itself in Rose's life. And, blessed or cursed with the ability to put himself in someone else's shoes and walk around in them for a while, he saw for the first time Danny McQuinn through Rose's eyes.

A more than averagely handsome policeman with a more than average dose of Irish charm, easy with women of all classes and all ages. A man an impressionable schoolgirl could very easily fancy that she was in love with—

He stepped forward sharply. McQuinn looked up, once again the dutiful officer, sprang to his feet.

117

'I was on my way back from Priorsfield, sir. As I was passing the house, I thought you'd better see these.'

Faro said nothing and held out his hand for the list containing the servants' names.

Without looking at his daughter, he said: 'Thank you, Rose. You may leave us now.'

His stern expression cut short any leave-taking between the two and as the door closed McQuinn said: 'These are the only two that need concern you, sir. I've whittled them down to the butler Gimmond, who has been there longest. You've met him. I don't think he could be our man.'

'And the other?'

McQuinn frowned. 'The only possibility would be the stableman who is also the coachman, Jock.'

'The man we met at the scene of the accident, of course.'

'Except that if he'd been guilty he would hardly have been lingering about the place.'

'He might have wanted to make sure the old man was dead.'

'True enough.'

'What do we know about him?'

'Not a great deal. Came from Colinton way about a year ago. Good references and all that sort of thing.' McQuinn looked at him. 'I know what you're thinking, sir, but he's a bit nondescript to fit the description of the missing heir. I mean, they're a well set-up handsome lot of men, you must admit that. And no one would call Jock prepossessing. He's a shambling sort of cove, what we call shilpit-lookin'.'

Jock the stableman certainly seemed an unlikely candidate, unshaven and distinctly unkempt. Yet that could be a disguise in itself.

'Remember he has been away from home for twenty years – if he is our man – and a lot of physical changes could have taken place. Again I put to you, McQuinn, that employers only glance at their servants. They have only minimal conversations and from what I've seen even avoid any kind of contact.

118

'Let's consider opportunity. Tampering with the wheel of Moulton's carriage was easy. And what was to stop him creeping up into the house when everyone was upstairs asleep and administering the fatal dose to the wine bottle? All he had to do was open the door, the men's chairs were at the fire, they had high backs which are meant to protect them from draughts – and the presence of whoever is serving them.'

'You think he intended to poison both of them, sir?'

'I do.'

'But why? What had he to gain?'

'Revenge now seems the most likely motive. I think he intended to get rid of both of them, then disappear. Who would be likely to check a servant who takes off? Then when the noise has all died down he would make a second spectacular reappearance as the heir to Langweils returned from America.'

McQuinn sighed. 'You make it sound very feasible, sir.' He grinned. 'But then you always do. However, there is one more thing. You asked me to get the servants to try to remember anything unusual about the happenings on the night of Mr Cedric's death?

'Well, we may have something,' he continued, excitement creeping into his voice. 'Seems Mrs Gimmond always counts the glasses when they are brought down for washing. They are real crystal and valuable and the master is very particular about them, especially as there are always extra glasses on the side table during a dinner party in case the guests wish to sample other kinds of wine or spirits.

'As I've said, they are carefully counted afterwards and any breakages have to be paid for out of their wages if any go a-missing. Well, on the morning of Mr Cedric's death, Mrs Gimmond was upset and with the house in uproar, she almost forgot about a glass that had been put out without Gimmond noticing that it was badly chipped.

'Mr Theodore had admonished him—'

'What happened to the glass?' demanded Faro.

'Mrs Langweil said she would take care of it.'

'Wait a minute – Mrs Langweil.'

'Yes, sir. Mr Theodore's wife.'

'I thought there were just the two men.'

'Apparently she looked in to say good night when all this was going on.'

McQuinn paused dramatically. 'I'm sure that something of the sort must have occurred to you, sir. That the poisoner could in fact be Mr Theodore's wife. Sure, she had time and opportunity—'

But Faro wanted to close his ears to McQuinn's logical deductions. So Barbara had been present. She could easily have – oh no. Not Barbara. Not Cedric's murderer.

'The glass, McQuinn,' he gasped. 'What happened to it?'

'I imagine it went out with the rest of the rubbish.'

Faro groaned. The one piece of evidence that pointed to the glasses and not the bottle having been poisoned.

If only Barbara Langweil had not been involved.

His gloomy thoughts were interrupted by McQuinn. 'Shall I check at Colinton village, on what they know about Jock?'

'Yes, do that.'

'What about the lawyer, sir? What are we doing about him?'

Faro had no reason except his own instinct for claiming that the old lawyer's death had been anything but an accident. A broken wheel on an ancient carriage.

He decided however that it might be worth looking in at the funeral. If only to have a few words with the clerk Mr Wailes.

He arrived at the cemetery just as the few mourners were leaving. As Moulton had been a bachelor with no family, he learned that Theodore Langweil had taken care of the arrangements and he wondered if there was any significance in this somewhat hasty committal.

He looked surprised to see Faro.

'Are you here in your official capacity?' he asked.

'I was hoping to have a few words with Wailes.'

'Wailes? Oh, yes. Moulton's clerk. His young clerk,'

120

he added with a laugh. 'Always gave us the impression that he was scarcely out of the nursery, therefore quite irresponsible. Must be fifty, if he's a day.' And looking at his waiting carriage, 'Well, he wasn't here to pay his last respects either.'

At Faro's look of concern, he said: 'Is there something wrong?'

'There could well be, sir. I went to the office after our talk the other night and the accident. I met Mr Wailes and asked to see the original of that letter from San Francisco.'

He cut short Theodore's angry retort. 'We have to check these things, sir, unpleasant though it may be. We cannot take anyone's word for what may be vital evidence.'

'Vital evidence? I don't know what you're talking about.'

Faro regarded him steadily. 'It has never occurred to you then, sir?'

'What are you talking about?'

'The possibility that your brother Justin might still be alive.'

Theodore looked at him as if he had taken leave of his senses. Then suddenly he exploded with laughter. So loud that people turned and stared at him, shocked by such mirth in this place of hushed voices and respectful silences.

'You'll be the death of me, Faro. Really you will.' And seizing him by the sleeve of his cape, he said, 'Justin is dead. Dead. Believe me, if you don't believe letters of proof.'

Pausing, he added: 'Well, did you see it?'

'No, I didn't. Wailes searched the papers and it wasn't there.'

Theodore shrugged. 'I expect he was looking in the wrong place.'

Maybe so, maybe not, thought Faro as they parted company at the gates. However, he decided to call on Wailes the following morning.

*

121

The office was now occupied by two young men who, presuming him to be one of the old lawyer's clients, explained that they were in charge and asked what they could do for him.

'It is Mr Wailes I wish to see.'

'We haven't seen him for several days,' said one.

'Not since he asked us to take over while he went to visit a sick relative,' said his partner.

'If you would care to state your business, we assist Mr Moulton from time to time.'

Faro shook his head. 'Do you have an address for Mr Wailes?'

As they searched in a drawer and eventually produced an address in Fountainbridge, Faro asked the senior of the two, 'And where does this ailing relative live?'

Puzzled looks were exchanged. 'Abroad somewhere, America or Canada.'

'No, Tom,' said his companion. 'That's where she used to live – you've got it all wrong.'

Faro decided to avoid the argument that was imminent. 'He left no address for this person?'

'Didn't seem to think that was necessary with us looking after things here.'

'He didn't talk much to anyone—'

And in a sudden rush of confidence his companion added: 'Certainly not to either of us. Kept himself to himself.'

'Very much so,' was the final pronouncement.

Wailes' address led Faro to a cheap lodging-house, shabby and none too clean. A woman wearing a dirty apron directed him grudgingly to the third floor up, left-hand door.

The stone stair smelt of mingled cats and human vomit.

As he expected, there was no reply and the woman was waiting for him. No, she hadn't seen Mr Wailes for a day or two. 'Hope he hasna' done a flit. Owes me two weeks' rent,' she added anxiously.

'Do you happen to have a key to the room?' The

122

woman nodded uneasily when Faro continued: 'Then perhaps you would be so kind as to produce Mr Wailes' key.' Faro held out his hand. 'Come along, now, I'm a police officer. We need to talk to Mr Wailes.'

'Och well, that's different.' The information seemed to cheer her considerably and leading the way upstairs rattling her clutch of keys she turned and asked excitedly: 'Has he done something, Officer? Never much to say for himself. Seems like such a nice quiet respectable-like mannie. But a body can no' be sure. It's the quiet-like ones is killers, I'm told—'

And throwing open the door she gave a scream of anguish.

Thrusting her aside, Faro rushed into the room, fully expecting to encounter Wailes' dead body lying on the floor.

To his relief the room was empty but even before the woman flung open the wardrobe and drawers it was evident from her wailing and her frantic manner that Mr Wailes had indeed done a flit, leaving his debts behind him.

Was there some other reason for his sudden disappearance apart from a sick relative? More important, was it connected with some vital aspect of the Langweil case?

Chapter Thirteen

Back at the Central Office, Faro put his findings to McQuinn, who asked eagerly: 'Shall we put out a warrant for his arrest, sir?'

'We can hardly arrest a man for debt just because he owes a couple of pounds for lodgings.'

'I realize that, sir. But it sounds as if this might be our man.'

'McQuinn, when you've been on this job as long as I have, the first thing you learn is never jump to conclusions, never try to force evidence that isn't there, just because it would conveniently wrap up a case. There's been too much of that already,' he added sternly. 'A history of innocent men hanged because the detective in charge of the case decided they were guilty and turned a blind eye to the evidence that they weren't.'

McQuinn looked surprised but impressed as Faro went on: 'You know my views or you should do by now. I'd rather have a guilty man go free than an innocent man hang.'

McQuinn shrugged. 'Sure, when you put it that way, sir. I expect you're right. So where do we start?'

'A few discreet enquiries at the Law Courts might save us a lot of embarrassment. After all, he might have had some quite legitimate reason for taking off suddenly.'

McQuinn regarded him doubtfully. 'Like what, sir?'

'We can't possibly answer that until we know a little more of his background. Think, McQuinn, there are a hundred different reasons for a man to leave his lodgings without being guilty of his employer's murder.'

McQuinn's expression suggested that he couldn't even think of one good reason.

'There must have been other people in Moulton's office too. Cleaners, messengers, for instance. God dammit, he must have talked to someone.'

McQuinn set off grumpily as Faro drew up the papers awaiting his return. To the known facts in the Langweil case, he added two further names.

The stableman, Jock. Was he known at Colinton? Could he be vouched for by family, etc.?

Moulton's assistant, Wailes. Had he absconded? Could he be vouched for by colleagues and acquaintances at the Sheriff Court?

Faro remembered faces very well. Neither man, he had to confess, had the least resemblance to the Langweil men, who bore a strong family likeness, nor by any stretch of imagination could either be transformed into the missing, presumed dead, brother, Justin.

Yet Jock and Wailes were the most likely – only – possibilities. There was only one thing bothered him about Wailes. In the unlikely event that he was Justin in disguise, then it would have been in his own interests to confirm that the real Justin died in California long ago. But his ignorance seemed quite genuine and Faro remembered how industriously he had searched for the missing document—

Faro shook his head. Perhaps he was on the wrong track altogether and he was making too much of a wild idea that the murderer was a missing brother, killing off members of his family as revenge for his young wife's death twenty years ago.

Before the possibility of Justin's existence, all evidence had pointed to Theodore. Or—

There was one other. His hand trembled as he wrote down 'Barbara Langweil', and he little guessed that within the next twenty-four hours, he was to discover that she had the best motive of all.

The information came his way quite casually, as did so many damning pieces of evidence.

That night the Edinburgh City Police held their Annual Grand Reunion at the Caledonian Hotel. This was a splendid occasion in which serving policemen and retired officers mingled together. The speeches were often long and tedious, but as compensation there was a considerable amount of ale and spirits, by courtesy of Langweil Ales Ltd.

There were for Faro many old and familiar faces and in the bar he was hailed by Peter Lamont who swayed towards him rather unsteadily.

'Good to see you again so soon, Faro,' he said slapping him on the back. 'Let's take a seat. Have a dram. Your young lad not here with you?'

Faro explained that Vince had been invited but was being kept rather busy at the moment.

Peter chuckled. 'Busy with other matters, eh?' And nudging him, 'That's a right bonny wee lass he's going to marry. Done well for himself, hasn't he?'

Faro agreed.

'I have to apologize for that business at the hotel the other day.'

'What business was that?'

Peter chuckled again. 'My missus put her foot right in it, she did.'

Before Faro could comment, Peter looked over his shoulder and leaned across confidentially. 'That business about Mrs Theodore being mistaken for Grace's stepmother.' He chortled. 'Did you not see me kick her under the table.'

Faro smiled. 'I don't think that would upset Grace. And it was a great compliment to her mother.'

'Her mother!' Peter exploded. 'That's rich.'

'I don't understand what you're getting at,' said Faro wearily.

'Of course you don't, lad. What I'm getting at is that the missus made a perfectly right assumption in the circumstances. You still don't get my drift, do you?' And when Faro shook his head, he said: 'You see when the two couples stayed with us in Perth, well, it was t'other way round. Cedric Langweil's missus was the young 'un. We both realized this when they came to the golf course. Naturally none of them remembered us. Visitors rarely remember the staff who serve them, much less the manager and his wife.'

Faro felt a cold chill steal over him. 'You must be mistaken.'

'Don't be daft, lad. Of course, I'm not mistaken. No one could mistake Mrs Cedric for Mrs Theodore.'

Faro knew with a sick feeling of despair that it was true.

'What I'm saying to you, Faro, is that Mrs Theodore spent the night with her brother-in-law.'

'What about the other two?'

'Oh, they shared another bedroom. They weren't going to be left out in the cold, were they now?' added Peter with a grin. 'Way the other half lives, it's all right if you're rich—'

'Are you certain?' Faro interrupted.

'Course I'm certain, the maid saw them in bed together.' Peter dug him gently in the ribs and chuckled again. 'Thought you'd enjoy that wee piece of scandal. Here, your glass is empty. Have another. One for the road?'

'Could your maid swear to this in a court of law?' Faro asked, conscious as he spoke that his lips were suddenly stiff and sore as if the words hurt.

'Of course she could. She's still with us. Happened twice, so she wasn't likely to have made a mistake—'

'Twice, you say?'

'Correct. On the two weekends they stayed with us—'

'Hello, you two – mind if we join you?'

As they made room for McIntosh and his guest, Faro heard little of the ensuing badinage. The party had suddenly gone sour on him, and making his excuses to the Superintendent he left shortly afterwards.

Back in Sheridan Place he did not wait up for Vince. He had no desire to impart to anyone, Vince least of all, the

127

new and damning evidence that had come his way.

It was unlikely that Peter would be mistaken, and if his chambermaid's observations were true then Barbara and Cedric had been lovers on at least two occasions. His righteous indignation did not extend to Theodore and Maud who had been similarly guilty.

It seemed impossible that those two unlikely people could have been involved in a passionate intrigue.

But Cedric – whom everyone loved. And Barbara. Barbara, his goddess.

As he fought with rising anger, he realized the necessity for calm consideration of this new evidence in the search for Cedric's murderer. At last, coolly, he recognized its significance. That it gave Theodore an excellent reason for murdering his brother.

It also provided a signpost to one of the most popular methods known to the police for a mistress ridding herself of an unwanted lover whose attentions were becoming threatening or embarrassing.

With considerable reluctance he underlined thickly: 'Barbara Langweil', on his list of suspects.

He slept badly that night and next morning he was still unsure how he was going to handle this new aspect of the Langweil murder. The *crime passionel*: for any policeman who has ever been in love himself and who understands the vagaries of the human condition, it is the crime in which it is the most difficult not to regard with compassion the slighted lover.

At the breakfast table Vince and Rose were chattering happily. Both addressed remarks to him which went unheard and therefore unanswered. They exchanged glances and at last Vince remarked upon his being unusually silent.

Faro tried to show an interest in this talk of weddings; through the murk of his own misery he was aware of Vince's happy mood, more relaxed than he had seemed of late.

He decided against drawing Vince into the further intricacies of this case, knowing that his stepson, strongly

128

influenced by love and loyalty to Grace, had his own most urgent personal reasons for believing with the rest of the Langweils that her father had taken his own life.

'September isn't too far off,' Vince was telling Rose. 'So much to do—'

Unfortunately for the couple's revised wedding plans, on the eve of Barbara's thirtieth birthday party at Priorsfield her husband Theodore and brother-in-law Adrian were poisoned.

Chapter Fourteen

Adrian was still alive.

By a miracle, he had taken the merest sip of the Langweil Alba liqueur when a commotion in the hall erupted to reveal Gimmond.

'Sorry to disturb you. But could Dr Adrian come quickly. One of the housemaids – upset a pan of boiling water—'

Before Adrian had finished attending to the crying maid and had dressed her scalded arm, he became aware of feeling distinctly ill. Leaving the kitchen hastily he vomited, retching with stomach pains.

Returning shakily to the scene he had just left, the door was flung open and Barbara rushed in screaming: 'For God's sake, Adrian, come quickly. Theo's lying on the floor. I think he's dying.'

'Get the carriage,' Adrian ordered Gimmond, and followed her upstairs where he took one look at his brother and decided that he had been poisoned. With Gimmond and Jock's assistance, while Barbara surveyed the terrible scene weeping and refusing to be parted from her husband, Theodore was bundled into the carriage.

Ten minutes later they delivered their now deeply unconscious burden to the Royal Infirmary. Jock, given instructions to alert Faro and Vince at Sheridan Place, found Faro alone.

The carriage hurtled towards Charlotte Square where Faro expected to find Vince with Grace. As he rushed past the startled maid unannounced, Maud appeared on the upstairs landing.

'Vince? He left about ten minutes ago.'

Faro cursed under his breath.

'Is something wrong?' Maud asked.

Faro considered and then shook his head. No point in alarming Maud at this juncture.

But at his urgent manner and distraught appearance, she said gently: 'Grace has not yet retired. She's in the library. She'll tell you if he was going straight home.'

Conscious that Maud was watching him very curiously, he ran lightly downstairs, and flinging open the library door he found Grace and Stephen Aynsley sitting on a sofa in the lamplight reading what looked like a book of poems.

Their heads were close together. Grace was smiling and Stephen's face, watching her, wore a look of complete and utter adoration.

They were unaware of his intrusion, like two people captured for ever in a romantic painting by the embers of a dying fire.

Faro felt a moment's anguish on Vince's behalf. Did he not realize that Stephen Aynsley, Grace's second, or was it third, cousin, was also madly in love with her?

Then the spell was broken, and they stood up to greet him.

'Vince? He went home, I think,' said Grace. 'What on earth is wrong?'

'Your Uncle Theodore has been poisoned.'

Grace gave a small scream of horror. Her hand flew to her mouth. 'No . . . Oh, no!'

'Adrian got him to the hospital. He wanted Vince to know.'

Maud had followed him downstairs. 'What is wrong?' she demanded. And leaving Grace to tell her, he fled leaving a scene of consternation behind him.

By the time he reached the hospital, Vince was already leaving the ward. 'Thank Heaven you got here—'

'Mrs Brook gave me your message—'

'How is he?'

Vince shook his head. 'I think this proves your theories,

131

fantastic as they seemed. It really does look as if the missing Justin must be somewhere around. There is no other logical explanation.'

But there was one, thought Faro grimly. Though, like me, you cannot face up to its grim reality. And at the light step behind them, he turned and looked into the tragic eyes of Barbara Langweil.

His mind was full of deadly accusations but now, even now, he turned away from them, determined with every doubt fading that he was going to see Barbara as innocent until the evidence proved her undeniably guilty.

There was nothing he could do here and he returned to Sheridan Place for what remained of that night of anguish and uncertainty, of dreams turned hollow, and goddesses who were but human after all.

At eight next morning he made his way to the hospital, but as he was entering the gates the Langweil carriage swept past him. Bearing a trio of weeping women, it told him even before he reached Theodore's bedside that he was already too late.

Theodore's death suggested his innocence in the murder of his brother Cedric and the questionable fatal accident to the lawyer Moulton who knew too much about the Langweil family.

He found Adrian, pale, dazed and sick-looking, staring down at the sheeted figure on the bed. Faro put his hand on his shoulder. At least he would survive.

Following him into the corridor, Adrian said: 'We did all we could. Dear God, who would do such a thing? When I think if we'd waited and opened it for the party – it might have been Freda. She has a passion for liqueurs.'

Faro looked at him. Had the amateur murderer got the wrong victim once again? Had Adrian's pregnant wife been the intended victim?

'Who would do this? Have you any ideas? For God's sake, Mr Faro, help us.'

Faro shook his head. All his theories – but one – had come to naught. 'Can you tell us exactly what happened before the maid came in and you had the glass in your hand?'

'Maud had left at ten when Barbara retired. We'd finished off the wine, and as it was well past midnight the servants had gone to bed. We were in rather high spirits, however, and Theo went to the cupboard and triumphantly produced Barbara's bottle.

' "She won't mind. Hates the stuff," he said as he broke the seal. "Shall we see if it's at the right temperature for tomorrow's party? Before Freda spots it. Then none of us will get a look-in." '

Adrian groaned. 'It's a family joke, just now; part of Freda's condition is a passion for sweet drinks.'

'Had the bottle come from the cellars in the usual way?' Faro asked.

Adrian looked embarrassed. 'No. According to Theo, it had been a present to Barbara, but liqueurs were far too sweet for her.'

Barbara again.

Faro groaned. 'I'm going to Priorsfield.'

'Do you think he might still be on the premises?'

'I think he might.'

'Then get him, for all our sakes. Get him, Mr Faro. Show no mercy. It must be one of the servants. It cannot be anyone else.'

Calling a carriage, Faro paused at the Central Office to collect McQuinn. Rapidly filling in the details, he waited for his sergeant's reactions.

McQuinn, now with the gift of hindsight, nodded eagerly. 'Always suspected something of the sort, sir. Amazed that you weren't on to it sooner. Are we to make an arrest?'

'The usual procedure, McQuinn.'

As the two men waited in the hall at Priorsfield, Faro gave the final instructions.

'Perhaps we're too late and the bird has flown,' whispered McQuinn anxiously. 'Shouldn't we—'

'No.' And as Gimmond appeared, Faro said: 'See no one leaves the house.'

133

He doubted he would be received by Mrs Langweil and was almost surprised when Gimmond led him into the library.

'If you will wait a moment, Inspector.'

'Before you go, Gimmond. You have heard about the master.'

Gimmond bowed, his face shadowed. 'Yes, Inspector. The staff are all devastated. He will be a great loss to us. A fine master—'

'You are, I take it, in charge of the cellar?'

'I am. That is solely my responsibility.' Faro's expression warned him of danger and he added hastily: 'There are, however, occasions when the master or the late Mr Cedric might take out bottles without my knowledge. They have their own keys.'

Faro looked thoughtful. 'And on the night of Mr Cedric's death?'

Gimmond frowned. 'I took out the wines required for the meal that evening from the menu prepared by Mrs Langweil and given to my wife.'

'And none of the bottles had been tampered with?'

'If you are implying that the seals had been broken, Inspector, I can tell you it would be more than my job's worth to put such a bottle out for the master's guests.'

'Then have you any idea—?'

A faint smile touched Gimmond's lips as he interrupted: 'Is this in the nature of an official questioning, Inspector?'

'No. I thought merely that being in the house at the time, you might have seen something unusual—'

'Or that I might have had a hand in it,' Gimmond concluded the sentence for him.

Faro regarded him with new interest. This was the first time Gimmond had ever referred, even obliquely, to their old association. And Gimmond had without doubt the best opportunity of all to put arsenic in Cedric's glass. Was it possible that the butler and his wife might be implicated in both murders? Could they have been the assassin's accomplices? Had he been too hasty in dismissing Gimmond from his list of suspects?

Watching him closely, Gimmond said softly: 'If you will cast your mind back, Inspector, you will recall that the verdict in my case was "Not proven". Otherwise I would not be in this position of trust, serving the family.' Looking at Faro, he said: 'I am not ungrateful for your silence, Inspector, especially where Sergeant McQuinn's enquiries are concerned. So if there is any way I can help you – you have only to ask.'

'Had Mr Langweil any enemies among the servants?'

'So you think it might be one of us? Now that would save a very nasty scandal, wouldn't it? Find a scapegoat below stairs.' Gimmond laughed mirthlessly. 'Typical police procedure, ain't it. Spare the rich master and blame the poor servant, if you can find one to fit the part.'

He sighed. 'You'll have your work cut out in this house, if that's your game, Inspector Faro. Ask Mrs Gimmond, if you won't take my word for it—'

'About this bottle of liqueur—'

Again Gimmond shook his head. 'None of us ever laid eyes on it. I'm told that Mrs Langweil had been given it as a present. So she said,' he added in mocking tones of disbelief.

Both men jumped when the bell by the fireplace jangled through the room.

'That'll be the mistress. If you will come this way, Inspector.'

In the upstairs parlour, Maud and Freda were consoling their sister-in-law.

Seeing him enter, they looked resentfully in his direction.

'Please, I wish to see Inspector Faro alone,' Barbara whispered. 'Please go, my dears. Of course I shall be all right.'

'Are you sure?' asked Maud. 'Shall I stay? I really would like to stay.'

'No, please go. And take Freda with you.'

Bowing the ladies out, Faro closed the door.

'Sit down, Mr Faro.' She smiled sadly. 'We have rather a lot to say to each other, have we not?'

She had been weeping, and weeping copiously. And

135

Faro marvelled how grief enhanced her loveliness, if that was possible, making her vulnerable and ethereal. More desirable.

An angel in tears. And yet this particular angel might he knew with dawning realization be a devil in disguise.

Suddenly his mind was cold and clear. He knew, and had known for a long time, but refused to admit it to himself, why the murders had been committed.

He could no longer cling to the hope, the faint possibility of a missing brother. Or a servant with a grievance.

All that remained was a beautiful woman with the most tawdry guilty secret of all. A lover who was her brother-in-law.

Faro drew a deep breath. 'Barbara Langweil, it is my duty to inform you that I am here to take you into custody for the murder of your husband Theodore Langweil—'

As he cautioned her he expected her to protest, to soften his heart with womanly tears, he was not kept long in suspense.

Instead she looked at him, dazed, shocked. Then she nodded.

'Yes, Mr Faro, I am guilty. I did it. I poisoned my husband.'

Faro said nothing. There wasn't anything he could say, hoping for a miracle, a denial of guilt with some totally unexpected revelation of damning evidence pointing to the real murderer.

But Barbara shook her head and sighed. 'It is not quite as you are imagining. It so happens that I loved Theodore, I shall always love him.'

And again she began to sob, while Faro stood by helplessly wondering, what then, if she loved him, was the motive.

'Cedric was my lover.'

That his suspicions aroused by Peter Lamont were true after all, gave him no sense of triumph. He felt faintly sick.

'It's a long story, Inspector. You must bear with me a little. I will try not to give way like this, but I will be honest with you.'

And so saying she straightened her slim shoulders and regarded him sadly. 'This whole sorry business began for me when Theodore married me, brought me to live at Priorsfield. Cedric and Maud were living here at that time and I soon realized, for he made no secret of the fact, that Cedric wanted me. He claimed that he was wildly in love and I, fool that I was, even flirted with him a little at the beginning. Naturally I was flattered that both brothers should love me.

'Theodore tolerated it with good humour at first. Then it began to irritate him and he suggested that Cedric and Maud make the move to Charlotte Square. There he thought Cedric's feelings would soon disappear when we met more rarely. But over the years what he regarded as a passing infatuation grew stronger. It became an obsession.'

Her face darkened as she continued slowly as if reliving the scene before her. 'While Theo and I mourned that we had no child as the years passed, Cedric was delighted. He said to me once, "If you had a child by Theo I would want to kill him. Yes, I would, my own brother. I could not bear the thought that he had given you something that I could not. That you could be possessed by him in a way that I could never possess you. Completely, utterly." '

Pausing, she glanced at Faro apologetically. 'I really believed until then that Cedric did not think that Theo and I – well, lived as man and wife. Once he said to me, "I would go mad if I let my mind dwell on Theo kissing you, holding you in his arms at night." '

'What about Maud? What were her feelings?'

'Oh, Maud knew. Cedric actually confided in her.' Barbara shuddered. 'But bless her good kind heart, she never took it seriously. She knew that I was utterly faithful to Theo and that I would never betray her. She had nothing to fear from me.

'And then late last year Cedric seemed unwell. He looked strange, odd. Then one day Theo told me that Cedric had seen a consultant. He was incurably ill. He was under sentence of death, as Theo put it, and had been given only a few months to live.

'As you might imagine, we were all shattered by this news. While Theo was the solemn, dependable head of the family, Cedric was so vibrant, the wit and humorist. They had always been close until I came along.'

She paused frowning and then added with a wan smile, 'I did love Cedric, you know. As I loved Adrian, for they were like the brothers I had never had. Then for a while, Theo seemed very preoccupied. I thought it was anxiety about Cedric which we all shared. I asked him about it and he said Cedric had asked him to grant a dying man's request.'

She was silent, staring into the fire so long that Faro whispered: 'Go on.'

She started as if she had forgotten his presence. 'It was – that Cedric had asked that he might share my bed for one night before – before the end. I was horrified. I thought Theo was joking. Then I knew he wasn't. He was almost in tears, my strong unemotional husband. "Do this for me, my darling." '

'I need not trouble you with my reactions to this monstrous suggestion or my tearful reproaches. How could Theo, my husband, even bear to mention such an idea to me. Did he not love me? And what of Maud? But Maud, it appeared, had been consulted and had given her consent.

'Reluctantly, after many sleepless nights, I gave mine. For Theo assured me that it would never change his love for me. He would love me more than ever for making this sacrifice for our beloved brother.

'Arrangements were made. We would stay at a small hotel in Perth where no one knew us. Theo had booked two double rooms under an assumed name. Cedric and I shared one, while in the other Maud had the bed and Theo slept on the sofa.

'On the journey there Cedric was so bright and excited, all trace of illness had vanished, he was literally like a young bridegroom. I could hardly bear to look at him. I felt physically sick at what lay ahead.'

138

Again she paused. 'I do not know that I can find words—'

Faro reached out, touched her hand. 'My dear Mrs Langweil, there is no need to tell me anything that does not relate to your husband's death – please do not distress yourself unnecessarily—'

'Distress myself!' she repeated, her face bewildered, dazed. 'That night with Cedric was like being with a madman. I did all he wished of me and yet it was not enough. It seemed that he could never be satisfied with what I gave him. He was like a raging animal. I was terrified of him, so different from my gentle, considerate Theo.

'At last dawn came. It was over. And we returned to Edinburgh. Theo never spoke to me about it and soon our normal life with all its social occasions and visits took over so that I would look across the table at Cedric and wonder if it had happened at all or if it was merely a very nasty embarrassing nightmare.

'And then Cedric became ill again. This time he was vomiting, terribly sick. He began complaining about bouts of indigestion but assured Theo that the consultant had said he would have these – towards the end. That this was part of the pattern, that his body was breaking up, its final decay.

'We were prepared for the worst. But even I was not quite prepared for what happened next. Theo came to me and said Cedric wanted one more night with me. This would be the very last, we all knew this. We could see that time was running out for him. But again I rebelled. I could not go through all that again. Never, never. But Theo took me in his arms and said: "This time, my darling, do it for me."

'And so, again, I agreed. Cedric wanted to go to a grander place, but Theo wisely dissuaded him. So we went to the same hotel, a quiet unassuming place where we were unlikely to be recognized, or even remembered, especially when the chambermaid came in and saw us in bed together.'

And Faro remembered Peter's piece of gossip and had

not the heart to tell her that indeed no one is safe anywhere from the hand of coincidence.

She had closed her eyes tightly, seemed to have difficulty finding words. 'It was as awful as before, perhaps even more so. And it must have been terrible for Theo and Maud too, although none of us has ever spoken of it. As for me, I told myself, it would never happen again. I had already decided that I would rather kill Cedric – or myself – first.

'But I was safe from Cedric. Three weeks later he was dead.' She looked at Faro. 'You will already have deduced that I had an excellent motive, the very best, for poisoning my poor infatuated brother-in-law. But I didn't, I swear it, although I might have been driven to it, had he not taken his own life.'

'Or was poisoned,' he reminded her.

'Poisoned?' Barbara's laughter declared such an idea incredible, absurd. 'Who on earth would want to poison Cedric? Except me. I was the only one who, God forgive me, hated him that much towards the end.'

She shook her head. 'But I didn't do it. That I do swear. Although I expect they will blame me, since I did poison my dearest Theo, and all because of some silly family scandal that Cedric was holding over him.'

She was silent and Faro asked gently: 'What kind of scandal could have been that important?'

'What indeed? I don't know the details. Only that Theo said: "If you don't do as Cedric asks, he has promised to leave with old Moulton something that will destroy me. That will finish this family for good." Those were his very words.'

'You have no idea what this was?'

She shrugged. 'I got the impression it was some kind of document relating to Priorsfield. But when I asked him to tell me, he just shook his head. "It's better you never know, my dear. This house was built on blood and now it's taking its revenge on us all. Cedric is dying. He has nothing to lose. But I have everything – everything." '

She looked at Faro. 'I haven't anything more to tell

140

you, Inspector. Are you going to arrest me? Am I to come with you now – right away? If so, may I gather some of my things—' And sadly, 'I don't suppose I will ever be coming back here, will I?'

As she stood up to leave, Faro took her arm. 'One moment. Tell me first, why? Why did you poison Theo? And most of all, why did you also attempt to poison Adrian, Adrian who has never harmed you?'

She laughed, shook her head. 'You still don't understand, do you? It was an accident. The poison wasn't intended for either of them.'

Pausing a moment, she added: 'Cedric left that bottle of liqueur with Theo the week before he died. "For Barbara on her birthday." Theo told me it was from a special batch but would need to be brought to room temperature if it was to be drinkable at the party.

'I opened the card in the sealed envelope. It said: "This is for you, my darling, in case I cannot be with you tonight. This will bring us together for always." Theo said it was a typical sentimental gesture by Cedric. But he seemed quite put out. We both were. It brought back memories we wanted to forget, blot out for ever.'

'Have you the note?'

'No. I burnt it.'

'Did anyone else see it?'

'Maud I think – I can't remember.'

'But you remembered the words.'

'I feel that I shall never forget them to my dying day. I see now what Cedric intended. On that last terrible night we shared together, he said: "If only I could take you with me when I go. I swear I will never rest in my grave until you lie at my side." '

At Faro's horrified expression she nodded slowly. 'Yes, Inspector. The poisoned bottle was meant for me.'

Chapter Fifteen

'Are we not taking her in?' asked McQuinn as Faro came downstairs alone.

Faro shook his head. 'I think not. The evidence is incomplete at present. Points to accidental poisoning.'

McQuinn whistled. 'You mean, she wasn't sleeping with her brother-in-law?'

'What makes you say that?' Faro demanded sharply.

McQuinn grinned. 'Plain as the nose on your face, Inspector. Surprised you weren't on to that straight away. Perfect reason for poisoning a persistent lover. When the murder enquiry looks like revealing all, she has to get rid of jealous husband who threatens to cut her out of the will. So he goes too.'

'You make it sound very simple.'

'You know and I know, sir, that most murders are.'

'What about Moulton, then?' Faro asked as McQuinn followed him out of the library and into the hall. 'Was that an accident?'

'We have no real evidence of murder.' As McQuinn spoke the front door opened and Theodore's two Labradors rushed in, closely followed by Barbara's maid. Calling them to heel, she hurried upstairs leaving a trail of muddy footprints across the polished floor.

Faro watched her go.

'What is it, sir?'

Faro shrugged. 'Perhaps you're right, McQuinn.' He pointed to the trail of muddy footprints across the floor. 'On the night of Moulton's death, we were very preoccupied by the seeming evidence that someone went out and that someone could have tampered with the wheelpin. Of course, someone was outside – probably Theodore himself – let the dogs out in the rain. As he did every night before retiring, an event so normal that he never considered it worth mentioning – if he even remembered it.'

As they walked down the front steps, McQuinn looked up at the windows. 'Are you sure we shouldn't be leaving a constable to keep an eye on things?'

'Very well. One of the lads in the carriage. Get him to stay.' As McQuinn opened the door for him, 'No, you take it. I'm walking back to Newington. Have some papers to collect from the house.'

'Sure, sir?'

'Yes. I need some fresh air.'

Considering that it was raining steadily, McQuinn's amazement was understandable.

In Sheridan Place, Faro went to his study, sat at his desk and stared at the Langweil papers. He wished the outcome had surprised him instead of merely confirming his worst fears.

There were still a few gaps but perhaps his meeting with Maud Langweil might throw some sense into his lost logic.

'Maud will confirm what I have told you,' had been Barbara's last words to him. Their painful interview over, he remembered how Maud had emerged from the adjoining room and had taken Barbara into her arms.

Looking across at Faro, she said quietly: 'We must talk. If you would care to call on me this evening . . .' Her frowning glance, a finger to her lips, indicated that Barbara was not to be further distressed.

Perhaps he was a fool, as his sergeant obviously thought, leaving a self-confessed murderess at large. Not only a fool, but a besotted one, putting all his faith into Maud Langweil's revelations, hoping they might bring about the miracle that would free her sister-in-law from guilt.

Faro presented himself at Charlotte Square at six

o'clock, in time to see Stephen Aynsley and Grace leaving the house. Stephen still wore that dazed expression of bemused love. As for Grace, she looked even more scared and bewildered than ever. It seemed that without Stephen's strong arm about her she might have collapsed. With a whisper of comfort, he helped her into the carriage, tucking the rug about her.

'I presume you are not needing us, sir,' he said to Faro.

'Not on this occasion,' said Faro with a hard look in Grace's direction.

She smiled at him wistfully. 'Tell Vince we expect him later this evening.'

Thoughtfully Faro watched the carriage depart. Of course, Grace loved Vince, his worries were nonsense. Possibly this was a situation she was used to dealing with, a bonny young lass who must attract many suitors.

And at that moment he had more pressing concerns.

Maud received him in the drawing room, her brisk manner indicating she was not to waste time on any preliminaries.

'You have my word that Barbara is innocent of Theo's – death. I read my late husband's note before she burnt it. What she told you is the honest truth. Do I surprise you, Mr Faro, that knowing about my husband and Barbara, I did not hate her? Nor him?'

She sighed. 'Barbara knew how much I loved him. And love him still.

'You may find that hard to understand. That a wife can remain in love with a husband who betrays her. You see, I realized that Barbara was only an obsession with him. I could forgive him that. As some men want power, Cedric worshipped beauty. He wanted Barbara for that alone. Not as a wife, not as a life partner. He wanted a goddess. Perhaps you understand that as a man.'

And Faro, who had taken a hearty dislike to Cedric Langweil since Barbara's revelations, was now guiltily aware that they had much in common.

Maud spread her hands wide. 'Compare the two of us. Any man who wanted to possess beauty would have chosen my sister-in-law.'

144

About to protest sternly that there were more important facets of womanhood than mere beauty, Faro saw
himself in the role of hypocrite. Offered a straight choice
between the two women he would have been less than
Cedric, for he would not have given Maud a second
glance.

'Cedric thought he loved Barbara,' Maud continued,
'and she destroyed him. Oh, she did not administer the
fatal dose, if that is what you are thinking. She was
innocent of that. It is as we in the family who knew have
always told you, Mr Faro, Cedric died by his own hand,
the victim of his lust for her.'

'Have you proof of this?'

'Oh indeed, I have,' she said sadly.

From her reticule, she took a small packet and handed
it to Faro. It contained white powder.

'This was Cedric's so-called indigestion powder. Take
it, have it analysed. I have already done so. Adrian will
tell you it is arsenic.'

'Surely you are mistaken. Adrian gave Cedric a prescription for indigestion.'

'Which he did not need and did not take.' She smiled and
shook her head 'An elaborate farce, Mr Faro, to create
the illusion in case any of us had suspicions. But allow
me to take you back to the beginning. Last summer there
were hints that Barbara and Theo were at last going to be
parents. We were all jubilant, all except Cedric. I shall
never forget his reactions. He was like a madman, mad
with rage. If Barbara had been his wife who had betrayed
him with another man, he could not have been angrier.

'I knew then that his feelings for Barbara, which we
had all accepted and teased him about all those years,
were no longer innocent adoration and admiration of a
young and lovely sister-in-law.

'Alas for us all, the baby came to naught. We were all
devastated. Except Cedric. He was jubilant, he almost
crowed with delight. When I said to him reproachfully
that having once conceived, it was possible that next time
– he gave me the oddest look: "Don't set your hopes on
it. It won't happen again. I shall see to that." '

' "What can you do about it?" I said. "After all, Barbara is your brother's wife." And I am afraid I lost my temper and added for good measure some reproachful words about it being time he put aside this silly infatuation that had gone on long enough.

' "Infatuation is it?" he said. "Perhaps you are right. Yes, it has gone on long enough. I see that."

'I was pleased, for it seemed that the first time I had been brave enough to speak up and show my anger had made him see sense. I wished now I had done so earlier, but I was always afraid that by doing so I might lose him.'

She sighed. 'I was never in any doubt about why he had married me. The Langweils needed my fortune at that time. But I loved him. He was all I had. And I told myself after Grace was born and the years passed happily enough, without too many enquiries on my part, that he did love me a little.'

She smiled and added sadly, 'In the same way as he loved his pet dog or the car. After my outburst, I was congratulating myself that our visits to Priorsfield were less frequent and when we were there he seemed less obsessed with Barbara. He treated her in an altogether more casual manner – oh, there were many small incidents that made me certain he had got over Barbara.

'And then he began suffering from stomach pains. He said it was indigestion at first. He was so ill that I panicked, called Adrian, who was very consoling, and said it must have been something he had eaten for lunch at the club.

'A little while afterwards he began to complain of increasing attacks of indigestion, and one night, when we were in bed. I saw him get up and remove something from the top shelf of the wardrobe.

' "What is that you are taking, dear?" I said. He looked round at me, so startled: "I thought you were asleep. This? For my indigestion, Adrian gave it to me. I am supposed to take a pinch every night in a glass of warm milk."

'I said, why didn't he keep it in a more accessible place, such as his dressing room. He got quite upset and said it was to stay up there out of reach of Grace, or me.

'I was amused by all these precautions and said we could always reach it by standing on a stool. He got frantic then and sat on the bed, said I was to promise, my solemn word, that neither of us would take any of Adrian's powder unless we spoke to him first. When I asked why, what was in it, he said it had been specially prepared for his condition and might do us harm, might make us very ill.

'As neither Grace nor I suffered from indigestion, I thought that very unlikely. I dismissed the whole incident from my mind for I soon had more important things to worry about.'

She sighed. 'It was about that time – one evening at Priorsfield – he told us that he had been attending a consultant and had learned that he was dying of a brain tumour.'

She paused, her eyes suddenly tear-filled. 'You know the rest, Mr Faro, for it is as Barbara told you.' Then in sudden embarrassment, 'You know, the weekends when he was allowed access to her.'

'What about the powder?'

'After Cedric died, I found it locked in a desk drawer in his study.'

'Wait a minute, Mrs Langweil, are you telling me that all the while he was supposed to be ill, he was in fact slowly poisoning himself?' asked Faro.

'That is correct. If wasn't until after he died that we – the family – guessed the dreadful truth. That he was never ill, never went to see a doctor. And we realized that he had been taking just enough arsenic to simulate grave illness. He knew about such things, for Adrian once told us it was rumoured that Napoleon took a pinch of arsenic every day to avoid being poisoned. And Heaven knows, there is always a plentiful supply in Priorsfield to keep the rats under control.

'Unfortunately what my poor husband did not realize is that it was possible to take an overdose for arsenic apparently accumulates in the system.'

And Faro, who thought he knew all about poisons from Vince, realized that had he not been led astray by this bizarre motive he too would have guessed the probable cause of Cedric's death.

'I had not the least idea what really happened. Like the rest of the family, I accepted his story that the side effects of his illness were these stomach upsets, which might worsen but could be held in check by Adrian's prescription.'

Again she paused. 'There was one incident that I see clearly now, but at the time I made nothing of its significance. One night he had been drinking rather heavily at dinner and had fallen asleep without finishing his glass of milk. I had toothache and as it was very late and I did not want to disturb the maids – they are up at six each morning – I went down to the kitchen to make myself a cup of tea and find some tincture of cloves. I'm a tidy person so I took Cedric's glass of milk downstairs and left it on the kitchen sink.

'Next day, Grace came to me in floods of tears. The maids had found her new kitten dead in its basket. I went downstairs to see what it was all about.

' "Something it ate," said Mrs Bates. "You know what cats are like. It gets nothing but good food here," she told me, "and milk too. When I came down this morning I gave it that half glass Mr Cedric had left. I don't like wasting good food." '

'I didn't want to distress Grace further by telling her that I had inadvertently poisoned her pet. And I had an uneasy feeling then there must be something very strong in Adrian's indigestion mixture to kill the poor creature, but when I asked him, he laughed. "Pure bicarbonate of soda, mostly." So I told myself that the kitten's death had been coincidence, something it had picked up in the garden.'

Faro felt he had to tell someone, and called in at Vince's surgery in the hope that he might still be there. He found him newly returned from a confinement and about to return home.

As they walked towards Sheridan Place, Faro related

148

the new developments: Barbara's story and Maud's evidence.

'Cedric wanted Barbara so desperately, he pretended to be dying as a last resort to sleep with her. He simulated illness by taking small doses of arsenic—'

'And he overdid it, of course,' Vince interrupted. 'He wasn't to know that it accumulates in one's system.'

'He killed himself and tried to take Barbara with him by poisoning the liqueur. And when his plan misfired, he almost succeeded in killing off his entire family. The Borgias couldn't have done better,' Faro added grimly.

Vince nodded. 'We should have believed them when they insisted that Cedric took his own life. They knew so much more about it than we did. He must have been quite mad, you know. Poor Grace,' he continued with a sigh. 'I don't know how she will take this.'

'I imagine the family will let her continue to accept that he believed he was dying.'

'That would be the best way. Certainly it will be my secret. She shall never hear the truth from me.'

But Grace was fated to hear far worse than that before the case that both men thought was closed had reached its final horrific disclosure.

Murders in the Langweil family were not yet over.

Chapter Sixteen

Guiltily aware that he had hardly seen Rose for the past two days, Faro decided to go home to Sheridan Place. He found Rose in the dining room.

'You have just missed Danny.'

For a moment he wondered who she was talking about. McQuinn, of course. 'He looked in about five minutes ago. Wanted to see you.'

'Was it urgent?'

'He didn't say. I was to tell you he was on his way to the Royal Infirmary. I tried to get him to wait and have tea.'

Smiling she poured out a cup for her father. 'Your Danny is almost as stubborn as you are. Did you know that?'

'No, I didn't.' Trying not to sound cross, he buttered a scone and said idly: 'So it's Danny now, is it?'

She nodded eagerly. 'Of course. I can hardly call him Sergeant or Mr McQuinn. He's a friend, after all.'

'And how long has my sergeant been a friend?' His tone light, Faro tried to sound amused while inside him anger stormed and roared and threatened to engulf that peaceful tea-table.

Rose looked away, still smiling. 'Since I was a little girl, lost in Edinburgh. You remember. He came to my rescue. I never forgot him.'

And Faro realized what he had never suspected. That ten-year-old girls make heroes out of mortal men. Had she thought of the young policeman all these years, seeing him not as her father did, as an irritating necessity of his life at Edinburgh City Police, but as a brave handsome Irishman? The thought was terrible, for he realized that never in all their years together had McQuinn been a person in his eyes.

'You don't like him, do you, Papa?' She sounded disappointed, sad.

'Of course I do,' Faro lied. 'He's a splendid fellow.'

Rose's look told him that his voice was too hearty and she didn't believe a word of it.

'I've known him for years and years,' he added defensively.

But Rose was too shrewd not to see through that. 'You mean, you've worked with him, but tell me,' she said, leaning her elbows on the table and regarding him solemnly, 'what do you really know about him?'

'As much as any senior detective inspector needs to know about a junior officer.'

'Such as? Go on, tell me.'

'That he's reliable. A good man to have around in a fight,' he added generously.

Her face told him that wasn't enough. Not nearly enough. That she regarded this as a rather indifferent testimonial of her friend's virtues.

'What do you know of his background, Papa? His early life in Ireland?'

'Not a great deal. As a matter of fact, he doesn't talk much about that.'

'You mean you know nothing? That you've never asked him?'

'Not really my business, is it?'

'As a policeman, perhaps not. As one human being to another, very much your business.' She paused triumphantly and then went on. 'Did you know that both his parents, two sisters and a younger brother died in infancy in the dreadful potato famine? And that the local priest had a sister who was a nun in the convent here in Edinburgh? They took him into their orphanage, educated him. You must know it, Papa. The Sisters of St Anthony, it's just down the road.'

151

Faro still went out of his way to avoid its gates.

Rose did not observe her father's shudder from the memory of what the sensational press referred to as the 'Gruesome Convent Murders'. One of his most successful cases, it was still unbearably painful to think at what cost to himself he had solved the murderer's identity. And he had reason to be grateful to McQuinn, who had saved his stepson's life.

He said, 'I thought he had kin in Ireland that he visited from time to time.'

'Cousins only. But he still regards Ireland as his home. He still yearns to go back there. It sounds a lovely country, Papa. I'd love to go there someday.'

Faro put down his empty tea cup, and kissing her lightly said: 'Who knows where your travels will take you, my dear. Well, I must be off again. I'll see you later.'

She followed him to the door and he turned: 'What now? You're looking very serious.'

'I'll tell you later, when you have more time.'

'More about McQuinn?' she asked smiling.

'No. Nothing more about him.'

At the Royal Infirmary, McQuinn was waiting for him. 'Piers Strong, sir. He's been attacked by keelies. Wants to see you urgently.'

As they hurried towards the ward, McQuinn filled in some of the details. 'He's not seriously hurt, just a bit bruised and knocked about. Fortunately he's got a good thick skull. Put up a good fight and one of our lads passing by came in the nick of time. One of Big Jem's gang. We've got the lad in the cells.'

Piers Strong, his head bandaged, greeted them wanly.

As Faro commiserated, saying they'd got the culprit, Strong shook his head. 'I think there was more to it than keelies, sir. I have good reason to think this was an organized attempt on my life.'

McQuinn and Faro exchanged glances. Those were the sort of odds where Big Jem was concerned. Those who hired him and his thugs paid handsomely for the risks run.

'Are you sure? What sort of enemies do you have?'

'I didn't think I had any. Now I'm not so sure. I understand that Theodore Langweil is dead. Is that true?'

When Faro said it was, Piers sighed. 'I can tell you this then, sir. He came into the office last week and said he wanted no further work done on Priorsfield and he wanted no archaeological revelations made public. Was that understood, he said. I wasn't sure what he was talking about and I said I didn't think there was anything of archaeological interest, more than that the house had been added to during the years.

' "That's what I mean,' says he. "I want your word that you'll keep any observations to yourself. We don't want to be bothered with investigations so I'll make it worth your while to be discreet." And he put down a purse containing one hundred guineas on my desk. I was taken aback, for I would have respected a client's silence without being paid for it.

'So I thrust it back at him. Said I had principles and all that sort of thing. And that if I thought something should be made public then all his damned money couldn't keep me quiet.

'He was furious. And so was I. And somehow that visit set me thinking. But it wasn't until I was hit on the head that it all made sense. He was so anxious that the wall in the small drawing room shouldn't be removed, or altered to make way for a bathroom next the master bedroom.

'And he lied and so did Cedric when they said nothing had been changed in their lifetime. You were there that night, sir. I was and am absolutely sure there was a door that had been covered in. The wallpaper gave the game away.'

'The wallpaper. Now I remember,' said Faro triumphantly. 'Of course you're right. It's too modern.'

When Piers looked puzzled Faro explained. 'I realize I was looking at it in a hotel Vince and I were visiting. The manager's wife said that it used to be fashionable twenty years ago.'

'That's right. I knew then the story about it not being decorated in this generation couldn't be true.'

Faro left very thoughtfully. McQuinn had called on Big Jem in his warren in Causewayside, and by dint of various threats for that gentleman's future which sounded feasible had got from him the admission that he had meant no harm, he had been hired to give the wee mannie a fright.

'He was very disgruntled, however. Because Big Jem likes to keep tabs on his hirers. Does a nice line in blackmail as we know already. Earns himself a few pounds. But this time, he was furious that the balance of payment on the job successfully accomplished would not now be forthcoming: "Hear that the mannie who got me to do the job is deid now."

'And he might as well have put Langweil's name and address into my hands, especially as we thought there might be some connection with Moulton's death too. Although Jem's better with his fists than pulling wheel pins out of carriages.'

When Faro drew his attention to the significance of those muddy footprints they had both seen in Priorsfield, McQuinn seemed disappointed.

'What do you make of it now, sir?'

'I'll tell you better when I've checked on a couple of facts.'

In Sheridan Place, Rose was awaiting her father's return.

'I have something to tell you, Papa.'

Faro was tired. 'Is it important? Can it not wait until tomorrow, my dear?'

She sighed. 'I've tried to tell you several times, but you didn't seem to be listening to me. I'm going back to Orkney, Papa.'

'What about your new school?'

'There is no point in my staying here until term begins, now that Vince's wedding isn't to be at Easter. I've had a letter from Emily. She and Grandmama miss me so much. And I miss them too. Anyway, I'm not at all sure that I want to go to the Academy after all,' she added bleakly.

'I thought you wanted to learn languages.'

She shook her head. 'I'm not sure about that any more. I'm not sure that it's a good idea of Vince's, that I should follow him into Langweil society when he marries Grace in order to find a suitable husband. From the few friends of Grace's I've met, I hardly think I'd find the kind of man I would want to marry in their ranks.'

'But you'll soon make friends at the new school.'

'I don't want friends, Papa. You don't understand, it's my own family I want. And you haven't time for me, really. Even less than when Emily and I come on holiday. If I stay here, we will get cross with each other. And I would hate that.'

'Aren't you exaggerating a little, my dear?'

'I don't think so. You won't – don't approve of people I like.' She looked at him. 'Like Danny, your sergeant. He's the only friend I'd want to have, apart from Grace. And I can see that Danny would become a subject of anger between us.'

'Danny McQuinn, is that it?' Faro exploded angrily. 'Of course, I'd object to your friendship – even if it were possible for a man nearly thirty to be friends with a girl of fifteen. I couldn't allow that and you know it. Especially as he is one of my junior officers.'

Rose smiled. 'Yes, it would be rather undignified for you, I can see that.' And leaning over, she touched his cheek and said softly, 'Poor Papa, you do see, don't you, that it is better if I go back home – to Kirkwall? Perhaps when I'm older, when you realize I'm not a little girl any longer, things will be different – easier for us. You will be able to treat me like an equal and accept the friends I want to make in Edinburgh.'

She was silent for a moment and he could think of nothing to say. Denial would be futile. 'If I stay here, I will only get fonder and fonder of Danny and you'll hate that.'

'Fonder and fonder! My dear, Danny is the first good-looking young man you have met. A pleasant change, no doubt, to the rough schoolboys you normally encounter, but do recognize it for what it is. That he has all the

155

excitement of being different, of living in a world that seems dangerous and strange to you.'

He took her hands and held them tightly. 'We all go through this phase in our lives when we are young—'

And not so young, his conscience whispered, remembering Barbara Langweil.

'It's called hero-worship.'

She sighed. 'Some call it love, Papa. And for some it lasts for ever,' she said sadly. 'Sometimes I have a feeling we never grow out of it, as you suggest.'

He could think of no answer that would not give her pain, and asked instead: 'When do you go?'

'Tomorrow.'

'So soon?'

'It's either now or the next boat – next week.'

He remembered there were only two sailings a week.

'But what about Vince – Grace?'

'I've said my goodbyes to Grace. She and Vince have known that I wanted to go home—'

And Vince had never breathed a word to him. 'A well-kept secret, eh?' he said bitterly.

'I wanted to tell you myself. Besides we thought you had enough problems at the moment. And incidentally, they think I'm doing the right thing.'

And coming round the table she flung herself into his arms. 'Oh Papa, Papa, don't look like that. I'll be back very soon, I promise, even if I don't go to the Academy, Emily and I will come for our summer holiday as usual and for Vince's wedding.'

He slept little that night. To his other failures he added those as a father. He had wanted so much to have Rose by his side, but her ill-timed arrival had shown them both how dreams are better to stay where they are. When they can be taken down and dusted from time to time and replaced, safe and secure, intact, without ever encountering the rougher stuff of reality.

The frantic activities of the next weeks left little time for brooding over his failures. The inquest on Theodore

156

Langweil, his wife cleared of suspicion in his poisoning on the evidence of Adrian and Maud. Cedric had accidentally taken his own life but had attempted to murder Barbara Langweil.

A sensational case indeed where a dead man was guilty of the murder of his brother and the attempted murder of his mistress. Respectable Edinburgh was rocked to its very foundations.

Vince's main concern was for Grace. And for Adrian's future, which might now be blighted. The thought of that so-called indigestion powder which had figured so largely in Maud's evidence might give patients pause for second thoughts.

'Poor Adrian. Guilty by association,' said Vince. 'In a family like the Langweils, it just takes one scandal and the whole lot topple. I hope he's right about leaving Edinburgh and setting up practice on the Borders, possibly using Freda's family name.'

'What will happen to Priorsfield?'

'Hardly a suitable venue for a general practitioner of medicine, is it? Besides it is Barbara's home for her lifetime as long as she remains unmarried, then it passes to Adrian and his family. Neither she nor Maud will be poorly off and I gather there are plenty of eager buyers for Langweil Ales—'

'And for Priorsfield,' said Adrian later that week as the three men dined together, 'if I feel inclined to sell. Barbara is staying at Charlotte Square just now.'

'Maud is trying to persuade her that it would be a good idea for the two widows to share one house,' said Vince.

'I had a visit from Piers Strong. If I do decide to sell, then there are quite a few things needing attention first. The whole place is getting rather dilapidated.' Adrian smiled. 'He has some extraordinary modern ideas. I'd like to find out if there is a secret room. That could answer a lot of things, besides my childhood dream,' he added wistfully.

A bottle of wine later, Adrian twirled his empty glass.

157

'You know I think it would be a good idea if we visited Priorsfield and had a closer look at that upstairs parlour. Especially with your revelations about the wallpaper,' he said excitedly to Faro.

Vince was full of enthusiasm for the idea. 'A pity we can't go right away, but it's too dark now. The servants would have a fit.'

'Tomorrow, then. Are we agreed?' said Adrian. And as they parted, 'Maybe Prince Charlie's French gold is still there, after all who knows what we will find?'

But Faro found himself oddly detached from the prevailing mood of excitement, unable to dispel an ominous feeling of doom.

Chapter Seventeen

A pity that the secret room at Priorsfield could not have remained where it belonged, in the bitter past, Faro thought afterwards, regretting that he had added his enthusiasm to what had begun like a boy's adventure story search for buried treasure.

He began to have his first qualms, the first tingling feelings of disaster as he watched the wallpaper, that too-modern wallpaper, being stripped and the padding removed from underneath.

There were cries of triumph, excited laughter, when it was realized that this was not the broom cupboard Theodore had suggested. Instead it was the entrance to a lost room in the house of Priorsfield.

And at the last moment Adrian held the lantern high and Grace shouted: 'Come on. What are we waiting for? This is marvellous.'

Afraid of what they might find, Faro wished that Vince had not been allowed to bring Grace along. Unfortunately when Vince had made the arrangement to meet Adrian and Faro, he had entirely forgotten that he was taking his fiancée to dine at the Café Royale that same evening.

What more natural when he confessed the nature of this other so-important engagement to save himself from Grace's sulks, than for her to insist on accompanying him?

As for Faro, all he felt at that moment was an ominous dread at Grace's excitement and the suppressed high spirits of Adrian and Vince as all three men threw their weight against the door.

'Don't say after all this that it's locked. We'll never find the key,' wailed Grace. 'It'll have vanished hundreds of years ago.'

'They don't usually lock broom cupboards,' said Vince consolingly.

'Nevertheless, there is a keyhole in this one,' said Faro.

For a moment, they stared at each other, frustrated, baffled. Then Adrian turned the handle.

'It moved,' said Vince. 'I think it's just jammed. All this padding—'

Adrian produced a knife, which was then run round the door's edge. Again they put their shoulders to it. This time it yielded.

'Great! Great! It isn't locked.'

The door opened slowly, reluctantly, creaking against the dust and cobwebs that draped like a curtain or a shroud before them concealing its dark interior.

Adrian went in first, held the lantern high. They were in a tiny dark panelled room, windowless. All light had once filtered through a small skylight, now similarly encrusted with the insect debris and cobwebs of ages.

Vince, with Grace holding his hand tightly, came behind Faro who was carrying a candelabra.

Blinking until at last their eyes grew accustomed to the gloom, Adrian's lantern revealed other things. That this room had been inhabited. There was a table with a plate on it, a chair. Even a small fireplace in one corner.

'Open the door as wide as you can,' said Adrian, gasping, seized by a fit of coughing.

'You can hardly breathe in here,' said Vince.

'Light,' said Adrian. 'We need more light.'

'I expect it was a priest's hole,' said Grace. 'I can't imagine anyone else living in such a wretched room.'

That was true, for everything was mouldered over with dust and insects, and the ancient odours of decay.

'Smells like an old crypt, doesn't it?'

Grace gave a little scream for there was another sound now. Rats. Rats scuttling, secret-moving, disturbed by this human invasion of what had long been their undisputed territory.

'And what have we here?' Against one wall was a chest. Adrian wiped the top with his sleeve. Once the dust settled and the cobwebs faltered, it was revealed as a very large and ancient oak chest, about six feet long, carved with symbols from another age.

The four stared doubtfully at this elaborate addition to the shabby rickety furnishings of the room.

'Open it,' said Grace. 'Go on.'

'Let's hope it contains the Frenchman's treasure,' said Adrian.

'Oh, wouldn't that be wonderful?'

At first the lid would not yield. Again came the question of it being locked. In the lantern, the candle was burning low.

'No, I think the hinges are rusty—'

The three men, with some considerable difficulty, succeeded in raising the heavy lid.

The lantern was set on the floor and Grace, who had been given the candelabra to hold, held it high. Then her screams rang out as she almost dropped it, the hot wax hissing on to the floor.

There was no treasure.

Only a decomposed body.

For a moment, Faro hoped that this was the legendary Frenchman who had disappeared in mysterious circumstances after a rendezvous he had failed to keep with Prince Charles Edward Stuart.

But the sweet smell of decay belonged to a later age and the mummified atmosphere of the casket had kept most of the dead man's clothes intact. Modern clothes they were, and there was enough hair remaining on the skull, enough withered flesh to be still recognizable as the Langweil strain.

The mystery of Justin Langweil's disappearance was solved at last.

The grim discovery pointed again to murder. But this time there were no suspects, for the answer was all too obvious.

Theodore Langweil had lied. There had never been a

letter from San Francisco telling him that his brother had been killed by renegade Indians. For Theodore had undoubtedly murdered his elder brother, with or without the help of Cedric.

And Faro found himself remembering that fatal evening when Cedric was poisoned, how he had overheard a conversation between the two brothers, Theodore adamant against Piers Strong's plans for a bathroom, and the atmosphere of menace he interrupted.

He never quite remembered how they quitted the room, Vince clutching the sobbing, frightened Grace. Or how they raced downstairs as if the murdered man might rise from his tomb and point a withered finger— But at whom?

They ran like frightened fugitives into the night where in the darkness of the drive the carriage waited to carry them back to safe surroundings, to normal life where such things as they had just witnessed belonged in the realms of fantasy, in the nightmares of Edgar Allan Poe.

Faro had not yet retired when Vince, having seen Grace and Adrian home, arrived back at Sheridan Place.

'It did happen – tonight, I mean, Stepfather. All the way back I've wondered if I dreamed it. Of all the awful things that have happened to the Langweil family, this is undoubtedly the worst. My poor Grace. She knows, must know, that her father was involved in her Uncle Justin's murder.'

'With both men dead, we may never know the whole truth,' said Faro. 'However, I've been thinking about that, realizing that Barbara gave us the answer. Don't you remember what I told you? She said that Cedric had promised to betray a family secret that could destroy them all, if Theodore couldn't persuade her—'

'I'm glad they are beyond the reach of the law, Stepfather, and that the family can be spared this additional horror. I presume it does not need to be made public,' Vince added anxiously.

'The skeleton of an unknown man was found behind a

162

blocked-up door in Priorsfield,' said Faro. 'Is that what you have in mind?'

Vince sighed. 'It doesn't sound very convincing, but surely you agree that the family have suffered enough?'

Faro's comment was: 'We know only that a murder was committed, twenty years ago, by person or persons unknown. Information to be filed away as another of Edinburgh's unsolved crimes.'

'Personally, I am more than happy for it to remain so,' said Vince. 'I think this is one time when we might let the past bury its dead in decorous silence.'

And so it might have done, had not Wailes, the lawyer Moulton's clerk, returned to Edinburgh after a prolonged absence. A mercy call on a sick elderly aunt in Yorkshire had extended into weeks instead of days. He had just returned to his lodgings to have an irate landlady report that besides owing her rent, the police were investigating his 'disappearance'.

Settling his debts with some alacrity, he presented himself in Faro's office, very anxious not to be regarded as a criminal. Distressed to hear of Theodore Langweil's death he announced that there were various family documents for Adrian as next of kin.

'Surely his widow is next of kin.'

Wailes shook his head. 'The document I have in mind predates his second marriage. Since there have been certain er, difficulties I gather, perhaps you would care to be present—'

They met in the doctors' consulting rooms, where Wailes handed over a large envelope that Faro had seen before.

'To be opened by Adrian Langweil in the event of the death of his brothers, Theodore and Cedric.' It held their two signatures and the date 1855.

Adrian had also requested Faro's presence, for he was even more eager than Vince to keep quiet any further family scandal.

The letter began:

This is to confirm that Justin Langweil, our eldest brother, died by our hand on the 26th day of February, 1855.

There was a horrified gasp from Vince and Wailes. Adrian paused before continuing.

Mr Moulton will confirm that Justin was unstable and suffered from moods of extreme violence which necessitated keeping him under restraint—

'A pity that Mr Moulton isn't here any longer,' Wailes interrupted briefly.

We had long suspected that he was insane and getting steadily worse. We were at our wits' end what to do, not caring to face the publicity and scandal of having a madman as head of our long-respected family. The effect on our thriving business would have been disastrous. When he was sane he was genial and helpful, but these lucid bouts were becoming rarer. So we put it about that he was an invalid, which meant that his occasional withdrawals from society (locked in an upstairs room) could be accounted for. Although on such occasions we were careful not to entertain or have any other than family visitors who knew and understood our problem.

Then during one of his better periods he escaped our vigilance and disappeared – we later learned to Glasgow. He had often stated that he wished to leave Scotland and go to America, certain that the climate of California would improve his health.

When several months passed by, we imagined that he had left the country. Imagine our surprise when one day he walked in, with a wife. A pretty young servant lass from Hamilton who he had met during his wanderings in the Highlands.

We rejoiced to see him looking so fit and well. Obviously marriage was the answer to his problems, we told each other. But not for long. Suddenly the violent attacks were renewed. This time they were directed against his helpless wife. In one of these rages, for he was very strong, he struck her and she fell from the balcony on to the terrace.

She could never have survived such a fall. She was dead and he had murdered her. But he was without remorse. With some considerable difficulty we locked him in the small room, once the withdrawing room of the master bedroom. With its skylight roof, we felt he was safe and could do himself no harm.

And there we proceeded to look after him, keeping his presence secret from the outside world. Sarah's death was dismissed as suicide, and we maintained Justin was too grief-stricken and dangerously ill himself to appear at the family funeral. When it was over we were faced with the terrible decision, whether or not to have him committed to an asylum. Obviously we could not minister to his needs indefinitely or keep the servants in ignorance of what was going on.

Once we went in and found him semiconscious. He had been beating his head against the stone wall. We do not know to this day which of us spoke the words which had been growing in our minds, the monstrous decision that had to be made.

He had murdered his young wife. He was guilty and for the sake of the family and the continuance of our good name, we must be his executioners.

The sentence once pronounced, we realized it must be carried out quickly before we could suffer any change of mind. So that night when he was abed we took in a pillow and both of us smothered him while he slept. Then we put his body in the chest where you will find it behind the door in the wall of the upstairs parlour.

Afterwards we blocked up the door and hired a firm from Arbroath to repaper the walls.

We did this woeful deed to protect you, our youngest

brother and the survivors of this family who now read this document.

Using the considerable influence of the Langweil name and the discretion of the Edinburgh City Police the murder of Justin Langweil was kept out of the newspapers.

It seemed that there was nothing more that could happen. There remained only the domestic details brought about by the earlier bereavements. Barbara and Maud, the two widows. Would Maud persuade Barbara to remain with her at Charlotte Square once Grace and Vince married?

Grace and Vince.

But here again, was the unexpected for which Faro was quite unprepared.

Chapter Eighteen

Some two weeks after Justin Langweil's remains had been placed with those of his ancestors in the family vault, after a short service of committal conducted by the Reverend Stephen Aynsley, Faro arrived home one evening to find Grace awaiting Vince's arrival.

Before Faro could exchange more than a dozen words with Grace, Vince appeared, and, leaving the young couple together, he went upstairs to his study.

There was a letter from Rose. He was reading it eagerly when a tap on the door announced Grace.

'Will you please come down, sir? I have something to tell Vince and I would like you to be there.'

Vince was leaning against the mantelpiece, smiling but quizzical, delighted to humour her. 'What is this great secret you are about to impart, my dear?'

Grace winced visibly. 'It is no great secret, and I thought perhaps it was one you might have guessed already.'

Walking over to Vince she took both his hands and held them tightly. 'My dear, I am sorry, but I cannot marry you. I am asking you to release me from our engagement.'

Vince's laugh of astonishment was a little hoarse. 'You are teasing us again, aren't you? Say you are, silly girl. Of course I won't release you. What nonsense is this?'

'It's not nonsense. I only wish it were. I have thought of nothing else for the past weeks, ever since – that night at Priorsfield.'

'What difference can that make? Justin's dead and

buried,' said Vince angrily, and looking at her stony face, he added: 'It's a bit thick, you know, concealing all this from me. I thought you were merely preoccupied with the wedding arrangements.'

'Please, please, Vince. Don't make it any more difficult for me. I cannot marry you. I now know that I can never marry you.'

And turning to Faro, she said: 'Surely you understand the reasons why and can convince him that in view of the recent disclosures about my family, I cannot marry him. Indeed, I am not fit to marry anyone,' she added sadly.

'I don't see—' Vince began.

'Then you should,' she said hardly. 'You are a medical man. Don't you understand I am the daughter of a murderer, the niece of a murderer as well as a madman? For pity's sake, Vince, I am not only ruined by my blood but by marrying you, I would ruin you too.'

'Rubbish,' Vince protested.

She shook her head. 'It is not rubbish. I only wish it were. Adrian has told me how we pass things on to our children, not only blue eyes and golden hair but traits of character. Good things, talents, and bad things too. Adrian is older than you, my dear, more experienced in such matters and I trust his judgement.'

'I thought he liked me—'

She seized his hands again. 'Of course he does. And that is the very reason why he believes my decision to be right. He believes that you have a great future before you.'

'A future that means nothing without you.'

'All right. If you won't think of yourself. And me. Think of our unborn children. What if we had a son and he took after my Uncle Justin, my Uncle Theodore, or even his own grandfather? Or a daughter? Lovely but mad. What then, how long then would love last? How long before we were not blaming each other for having begot such monsters? Oh Vince, Vince, for pity's sake—'

As she fell into a chair, her slim shoulders racked with

168

sobs, neither man moved to comfort her, both stared down at her and then at each other.

Faro knew that she spoke the truth, as Vince would. Some day, but not now. That knowingly endangering a future generation with family madness was the one unforgivable sin. For madness was like ripples in a still pool. It was not only those nearest it affected but all in its orbit.

And Faro remembered Sarah the gentle wife who had been struck down and killed by her husband in his temporary madness.

At last Grace looked up, wiped her eyes. Rose to her feet and regarding them sadly, removed Vince's ring from her finger.

'Keep it,' he said harshly.

'No—'

'Keep it. To remember me by.'

'I need no ring for that,' she said, her eyes welling with tears. 'I shall never forget you, never. I shall always love you, Vince.'

Vince rushed forward. 'Then forget all this. Marry me. And to hell with the future. We needn't have children. Then all your arguments are futile.'

'No. We both love children. Marriage for us would be a farce without them. And if I were your wife I would want your child.' And pulling away from him, she said: 'I have made my decision.'

'What will you do?'

'I am going to Africa.'

'Africa! For God's sake—'

'Yes. With Stephen.'

'Stephen? Your cousin?'

'I am not going to marry him. Believe me when I tell you that I am not to marry him or anyone. He is not your rival, so don't look like that, Vince. But by going away from Scotland I can serve some useful purpose in the world. I can sort out my feelings—'

'Promise me something then—'

'Of course.'

169

'Promise me that if you ever change your mind you will come back to me.'

Grace smiled. 'There is no other man I would come back to. You have my word on that.'

'Then give it a year, two years. And if by the end of that time you still want to be my wife, I will be waiting. I promise—'

Faro went out and slowly closed the door. He could no longer bear to witness the sufferings of the young couple whose happiness was dear to his heart.

Instead of fulfilment and joy, what he had dreaded had happened. The evils of the Langweil past had caught up with them and Grace was right too. For not only caught up but overwhelmed, the guilty and the innocent alike. And he thought of that unborn baby, the child of Adrian and Freda who would carry on the Langweil strain. At least Adrian and Grace were guiltless of bloodshed, but who could tell what repercussions lay in store for future generations, if as Adrian suspected evil as well as good could be inherited.

The Langweil case was almost closed. There were no more revelations to destroy them. He had one last call to make.

He was going to Priorsfield, where Barbara Langweil was waiting for him.

'Adrian will have told you that I am leaving Priorsfield.'

Barbara smiled sadly. 'This is a house of sad memories. I still cannot believe that I lived here for twelve years with a man I loved so deeply, and never knew or suspected the terrible crime he and Cedric had committed.'

She paused. 'Do you think it is possible to love that much, and yet never know a secret like that? And yet if he were to walk in the door this moment, I would do the same again. I would do more, I would lie and cheat to save him from the gallows. That is the kind of woman you see before you, Mr Faro. With few moral principles, alas, beyond the workings of her own heart.'

'When are you leaving?' he asked.

Gesturing towards the already shrouded furniture, she

said: 'As soon as I have made the final arrangements.'

'You do not care to stay with Maud then?'

'Without Theo my final link with Edinburgh – and this country – is broken. Although I might live here in Priorsfield in comfort for the rest of my life, what kind of life would that be, I ask you, Mr Faro?'

He could think of no reply.

'I am thirty. I still have, with good health and barring accidents, half of my life before me.'

Looking round the room, she stood up, gathered her shawl from the chair. 'This room depresses me. Too many memories. I still see Theo everywhere. Let us go into the garden. The roses are blooming. They are such cheerful flowers, I find it impossible to be sad among roses.'

Faro walked at her side, conscious of that lovely presence, but aware that he knew her not one whit more than when he had fallen in love with her on his first visit with Vince and Grace.

He had imagined that grief might have changed the perfection of that countenance, might have made his goddess into an earthbound creature—

She walked swiftly for a woman with long-legged, easy strides. 'I am going back to America,' she was saying. 'I have a little money of my own that Theo left me, and with it I shall start afresh, a new life. Somewhere, I'm not sure where yet.'

'What will you do? Have you any plans?'

'I haven't decided yet, but something will come along, I'm sure. I have friends – humble but good – who will help me make the right decision. I have no one here. No one I care for.'

And her words blotted out the sun from his world, and what he had been going to ask her. To be his wife. The very reason for his coming to Priorsfield died on his lips. As if ice had been carried on the light summer breeze that stirred the perfume of the roses around them.

Trying not to sound wounded he said: 'You must not feel uncared for. You have people here who care and who will miss you.'

She looked at him in amazement as if such an idea had

171

never occurred to her. Taking a moment to answer, she said slowly: 'I dare say you are right. Yes, of course, you are. And you are a very kind man, Mr Faro, a very nice person in spite of being a detective.'

Was that how she thought of him? And Faro, who never cried, felt the prickle of tears behind his eyes. All that love and suffering on her behalf. All his dreams about her and she was totally unaware that he was more than 'a nice person'.

Such fools we are, such fools, he thought.

Suddenly, he stopped, and turning her to face him, he took her roughly in his arms. Held her, savouring the sweetness of the moment, of that slim firm outline of her body so close.

Prepared for resistance, there was none.

Acquiesence then? His heart hammered hopefully.

Did that mean—?

He looked into her face. She was smiling, politely, enigmatically. It was as if he had taken into his arms, in a surge of passion, one of the white marble statues that surrounded the paths and wore the same curiously blood-less expressions.

Embarrassed now, he released her. There seemed nothing more to say and both hastened their steps towards the iron gates at the end of the drive.

As they parted there for the last time, she held out her hand and then, as if she changed her mind suddenly, she stood on tiptoe, took his face in her cool slender hands and kissed him lightly on the mouth.

'Goodbye, dear kind Inspector Faro. And thank you.'

He touched his lips in wonder. But when he turned round, she had gone. Vanished. Only the roses nodded and the garden was empty.

Walking back along the road past Duddingston he remembered Rose's letter, that she sounded happy, content to be back in Kirkwall with his mother and Emily, surrounded by all that was familiar to her, by loves that were not touched by uncertainty.

172

And he remembered her words to him as they waited on the dock at Leith for the Orkney boat to leave.

'You were very lucky never to have loved anyone but Mama, so that you can be happy enough with those memories not to need to search for anyone else to replace her.'

He had looked at his daughter. Yes, he would let her believe that, although it wasn't true, and some day, when she was older and happily married with a string of bairns clutching at her petticoat, he might tell her the truth.

About Barbara. And all the others he had loved and lost. Or who had loved him and he had hurt by turning away.

'Do you mind Barbara Langweil?' he'd begin. And he'd see her eyes widen in surprise as he told her of this day, and his last visit to Priorsfield.

And how for some men, it's a lifetime of loving, for some only a butterfly kiss from a goddess in a summer rose garden.

The Langweil case was over, the players in its drama had departed, its stage was empty for all but the few innocents bruised by its impact.

And heading towards the Central Office, as he had done for so many years, and the next case that was waiting for him, he remembered one indisputable lesson life had taught him. Broken hearts are seldom fatal. That given time and patience they invariably heal.

He mustn't abandon hope. Without hope life was indeed a derelict wasteland.

Hope for a daughter that the pangs of first love would heal. Hope for Vince that his beloved Grace would return to him one day and together they would mend their broken lives that had been the Langweil legacy. Hope for himself, for that hazy unknown future and a final confrontation and outwitting of a master criminal.

'The evil that men do lives after them.' So Shakespeare had said. A truth that still remained unalterable and would continue to remain so until man and time itself were no more.

173

Note to Readers

For those interested in Inspector Faro's earlier cases, the one referred to on page 63 is *Bloodline*; and on page 152 *Enter Second Murderer*, both published in this series by Macmillan Crime.